Kate Saunders worked as an actress until she was twenty-five and then became a writer. She is the author of six novels for adults and has edited one collection of short stories. For children, she has written the very successful *Belfry Witches* series, on which a major BBC TV series was based, and *Cat and the Stinkwater War*. As a journalist she has worked for the *Sunday Times*, the *Daily Telegraph*, the *Independent* and the *Sunday Express*. She can also be heard regularly on BBC Radio 4. She lives with her family (and three cats) in London.

The Belfry Witches

Kate Saunders
Illustrated by Tony Ross

MACMILLAN CHILDREN'S BOOKS

A Spell of Witches, Mendax the Mystery Cat and *Red Stocking Rescue*
first published 1999 by Macmillan Children's Books

This edition published 2003 by Macmillan Children's Books
a division of Macmillan Publishers Limited
20 New Wharf Road, London N1 9RR
Basingstoke and Oxford
www.panmacmillan.co.uk

Associated companies throughout the world

ISBN 0 330 42103 4

3 5 7 9 8 6 4

A CIP catalogue record for this book is available from
the British Library.

Typeset by SX Composing DTP, Rayleigh, Essex
Printed and bound in Great Britain by Mackays of Chatham plc, Kent

Contents

A Spell of Witches

For my son, Felix

1

Red Stockings

"It's not fair!" moaned Old Noshie. "It's the unfairest thing in the world!"

"How dare she say we can't go to the Hallowe'en Ball?" raged Skirty Marm.

It certainly did seem very hard. On Witch Island, the Hallowe'en Ball was the high spot of the whole year. There was to be drink, food, dancing, a bonfire and a real jazz band. But Old Noshie and Skirty Marm – along with all the other Red-Stocking witches – had been ordered to stay in their caves.

I should explain that on Witch Island, when a witch reaches the age of one hundred, she is given her red stockings and uses the Red-Stocking Spellbook. At the age of two hundred, the stockings become green and the spellbook is more advanced. Finally, at the age of three hundred, a witch becomes a Purple-Stocking and is allowed to cast the most powerful spells of all.

Just because Mrs Abercrombie, the Queen of all the Witches, had heard some Red-Stockings tittering behind her back, she had decided they were silly and cheeky and should be punished. Their Red-Stocking Spellbooks were taken away for a week and they were banned from the Hallowe'en Ball. All the Red-Stockings were furious.

"What a nerve," said Skirty Marm, "treating us like little Yellow-Stockings!"

The Yellow-Stockings were the baby witches, still at school. It was a terrible insult.

The fact was, the Red-Stockings were not very popular among the senior witches – especially Old Noshie and Skirty Marm, who were often rather saucy and disrespectful. These two had been best friends since Yellow-Stocking days. They were now one hundred and fifty years old, which is very young for a witch.

Skirty Marm was tall and skinny, with a wrinkled grey face, beady red eyes and a tangle of purple hair. Old Noshie was shorter and fatter. Her face was bright green and glowed in the dark. She was bald but wore a blue wig to keep her head warm. On Witch Island, no witch gets a cave of her own until she is a Purple-Stocking, but Old Noshie and Skirty Marm were happy to share and had already decided that they would always live together.

They had been looking forward to the Hallowe'en Ball for months.

"It makes my blood boil!" said Old Noshie. "Let's have a nice cup of warm mud to cheer ourselves up."

Skirty Marm, however, was far too cross to think of being cheered up. "I don't care what Mrs Abercrombie says," she declared. "I'm going to that ball – whether she likes it or not!"

"Don't be daft," Old Noshie said. "Think what she'd do to you if she ever found out."

All the witches of Witch Island lived in terror of Mrs Abercrombie. The Queen of the Witches was hugely fat and amazingly ugly – even by witch standards. She had pointed iron teeth, her chin was covered with grey hairs, and she had a dreadful temper.

But more than this, Mrs Abercrombie owned the Power Hat. The Power Hat was two metres tall and had a candle stuck in the point at the top. The flame of this candle never went out, and the Hat gave its owner great magic powers. Nobody dared to annoy the queen when the Power Hat was on her head.

"I don't care," said Skirty Marm. "We're going to that ball, and Mrs A. won't know a thing. Listen . . ."

Grinning wickedly, she whispered her brilliant plan into Old Noshie's green ear.

Old Noshie was doubtful at first, but she always went along with Skirty Marm in the end. In her Yellow-Stocking days, her school reports had said she was "easily led", and this was still true where Skirty Marm was concerned – Old Noshie thought her friend was the cleverest witch in the world.

Hallowe'en is the night when the witches of the island fly out among the humans. They upset television aerials, prod sleeping babies to make them cry, and generally do all kinds of bad things. It is the witches' favourite night of the year – but this time, it was quite spoiled for the Red-Stockings.

As they lined up to mount their broomsticks, they looked sadly at the football pitch, which was decorated with coloured lights and black

4

balloons, all ready for the party. Old Noshie and Skirty Marm, however, were in high spirits. They kept pinching each other and bursting into giggles, and nobody knew why.

It was a splendid night. Noshie and Skirty flew to a big city and made all the lights on tall office blocks spell out rude words. They went to a dairy and turned all the milk bad. They went to a flower market and changed all the flowers into mouldy cabbages.

At one hour past midnight, they landed on the black beach of Witch Island. The Hallowe'en Ball was in full swing. The football pitch was a

whirling mass of pointed hats and green and purple stockings. A gigantic bonfire filled the sky with a red glow, and the jazz band were playing wildly.

The Red-Stocking witches slunk miserably home to bed, pretending they didn't care. But Old Noshie and Skirty Marm rushed back to their cave, laughing so much that they could hardly stand up.

"Everything ready, Nosh?" asked Skirty Marm jauntily.

Old Noshie whispered, "Are you sure it will work?"

"Stop moaning," said Skirty Marm, "or I'll biff you. If we don't hurry, all the food will be gone – those old Purple-Stockings are such greedy pigs."

From under a rock she took two pairs of green stockings, which they had spent the whole afternoon dyeing in spinach juice. When they had put these on and admired their reflections in a puddle, they painted their faces so they would not be recognized. This was particularly important for Old Noshie, whose green face shone like a traffic light.

The moment their disguises were complete,

6

they ran out to the football pitch and threw themselves into the party. By now, the other witches were so tipsy that they hardly noticed these two strange Green-Stockings. Old Noshie and Skirty Marm hopped and jumped around the bonfire until they were breathless. Then they went to the food table and stuffed themselves with barbecued bats, salted newts' skulls and spiders in batter.

If they had been careful, they might never have been discovered. But it was at this point that the witches did a very silly thing. They grabbed a full bottle of Nasty Medicine and drank the whole lot between them, in five minutes.

Now, every sensible human knows you must NEVER, EVER drink someone else's medicine, because it is EXTREMELY DANGEROUS. But Old Noshie and Skirty Marm were witches, and all it did was make them disgracefully tipsy.

They looked over at Mrs Abercrombie, who was finishing a crate of Nasty Medicine single-handed. She was telling jokes which were not at all funny, but the crowd of Purple-Stockings around her had to laugh – they knew what a terrible temper she would be in the next day.

"It's time she was taught a lesson!" declared

Old Noshie. "Come on – it's my turn to have an idea for a change. I'll show her she can't squash us Red-Stockings!"

A few minutes later, the jazz band stopped playing and the lead singer made an announcement. "We're taking a break now while two talented Green-Stockings entertain you with a song. Here are the Bubbling Cauldron Stompers, wishing you a happy Hallowe'en!"

The crowd of witches clapped and whistled as a bald-headed Green-Stocking stepped onto the stage.

"My friend and I," she shouted, "will now sing a little song called 'A Nasty Old Thing'. Thank you."

Another Green-Stocking pranced onto the stage – but this time there was no applause. She had stuffed her dress with pillows to make her look very fat. She wore a false grey beard. Worst of all, she had a candle stuck in her pointed hat. The witches looked round at the queen, but Mrs Abercrombie was busy opening another bottle and had not seen the shocking figure on the stage.

In ghastly silence, the two talented Green-Stockings began to sing.

"Once there was an old witch,
O, harken to my tale,
She truly was a bold witch
And fatter than a whale.

Her chin was grey and hairy,
She snored just like a zombie –
O! Certainly no fairy
Was Mrs Abercrombie!"

A gasp of horror rose from the crowd, but the two Green-Stockings only sang louder.

"Her knees they were so baggy,
And (let us not quibble)
Her stomach was all saggy,
Her mouth was full of dribble.

From ten miles you could not miss her,
She's like a wobbly jelly –
I would not like to kiss her,
She is so Fat and Smelly!"

"Stop!" screamed Mrs Abercrombie. Her hideous face was as purple as her stockings. "How dare you insult your Beloved Queen?"

"Pooh to you!" smirked the two daring Green-Stockings.

"You'll be sorry for this!" roared Mrs Abercrombie, shaking a hairy fist. "What are your names?"

"Not telling!" shouted the two witches.

Mrs Abercrombie surveyed the crowd with a look that made them all tremble. "I want their names!"

Suddenly, one of the Purple-Stockings in the jazz band leapt onto the stage and grabbed Old Noshie by the ear.

"Look! This is a disguise – she's painted!"

"That's no Green-Stocking!" yelled someone else. "That's Old Noshie – I'd know her anywhere! And the other one must be Skirty Marm!"

"Arrest them!" bawled Mrs Abercrombie. "Throw them into prison! I shall try them tomorrow, in a Grand Court of Witches!"

"Oh, no!" wailed Old Noshie. "What have we done?"

And that is how Old Noshie and Skirty Marm committed the most terrible crime in the history of Witch Island.

2

No Stockings

"Silence in court," ordered Mrs Abercrombie. "Bring in the prisoners."

The Meeting Cave was packed. Every witch on the island had come to see the trial, and there had been fierce fighting for the best seats. The Yellow-Stockings – even little witches of only seventy or eighty – had been given the day off school. The Red-Stockings secretly felt rather proud of the two criminals, but the Green- and Purple-Stockings were furious.

When Old Noshie and Skirty Marm were led into the dock, the Green- and Purple-Stockings began to spit and shout and boo, and were only stopped by Mrs Abercrombie repeating, "Silence in court!"

There was silence at once, for the Queen of the Witches had never looked so terrifying.

"My subjects, last night, at the Hallowe'en

Ball, a shocking crime was committed against my sacred person."

"Woe!" cried the Green- and Purple-Stockings, "Woe to the prisoners!"

Old Noshie and Skirty Marm had their hands tied behind their backs, and they looked very sulky. They did not, however, look sorry for their shocking crime.

"Old Noshie and Skirty Marm," Mrs Abercrombie said, "you are charged with being at the Hallowe'en Ball without an invitation. You are also charged with unlawfully impersonating Green-Stockings, insulting your Beloved Queen – namely, me – and with being drunk and disorderly. Have you anything to say, before I find you guilty and punish you?"

"You were more drunk and disorderly than us!" said Old Noshie. "You had to be carried home."

"You are also charged with contempt of court!" screamed Mrs Abercrombie.

"Pooh to you!" replied the prisoners, sticking out their furry tongues at their Beloved Queen.

Mrs Abercrombie looked as if she would explode with rage. "Did you, or did you not, sing a

highly offensive song called 'A Nasty Old Thing'?"

"Yes," said Skirty Marm. "I wrote all the words, except the bit about you being fat and smelly – that was Noshie. We thought it was really funny."

"Funny!" gasped Mrs Abercrombie. "To insult *me*!"

"*Once there was an old witch*," chanted Old Noshie and Skirty Marm, "*O, harken to my tale – she truly was a—*"

Two Purple-Stocking guards stopped up their mouths with rags. The Meeting Cave was in an uproar. Several witches fainted with horror, and a dozen Red-Stockings had to be arrested for laughing.

"My subjects!" cried Mrs Abercrombie. "Are these rascals guilty or not guilty?"

"GUILTY!" cried thousands of witches with one voice.

"Right," said Mrs Abercrombie, "I will now pass sentence. And I will have such revenge as this island has never seen."

The crowd broke into murmurs of excitement. What would the queen do? The worst punishment on Witch Island was to have your broom broken in public, but there had never been a crime like this. Old Noshie and Skirty Marm were beginning to wish they hadn't been so cocky. They had decided they didn't care if their brooms were broken – but Mrs Abercrombie was looking ominously pleased with herself.

"Old Noshie and Skirty Marm," said Mrs Abercrombie solemnly, "you are sloppy, cheeky and disrespectful to your elders. You think you're going to get away with nothing worse than broken brooms – well, you aren't."

"No!" shouted all the older witches gleefully. "Certainly not!"

"If," the queen went on, "I have got my

14

temper back in a hundred years – which is VERY UNLIKELY – I may consider your case again. Meanwhile, for the crime of pretending to be Green-Stockings, you will be stripped of your red stockings for ever."

This was terrible. Old Noshie and Skirty Marm squealed inside their gags.

"And for the far more serious crime of singing that disgusting song, you will be banished from this island for one hundred years."

Old Noshie and Skirty Marm turned ashy pale. Banished! What would become of them?

The witches cheered Mrs Abercrombie out of the Meeting Cave, then surged away to listen to the highlights of the trial on the radio.

The two disgraced witches were locked up in prison until the hour of their banishment.

"This is all your fault," said Old Noshie. "I never should have listened when you made me gatecrash the ball."

"*My* fault?" shouted Skirty Marm. "We'd have been fine if you hadn't made me dress up as the queen!"

"We shouldn't argue," Old Noshie said, her green lip suddenly quivering. "We haven't got anything but each other now. Oh, Skirt, what's going to happen to us? Where will we go? Will we die?"

"I'm not going to die," growled Skirty Marm, trying to sound brave. "I wouldn't give Mrs A. the satisfaction. She'll be sorry for this one day, you mark my words."

When the night was at its blackest, Old Noshie and Skirty Marm were taken to the top of a high cliff and stripped of their red stockings.

"That'll teach you!" sneered the Purple-Stocking guard, waving the confiscated stockings in their faces. "You won't be so swaggering and cheeky now!"

Old Noshie and Skirty Marm had lost all their swagger and cheek. Now they were only cold and hungry, and very frightened. Struggling against the freezing wind, they mounted their broomsticks and flew out into the darkness.

Only a few hours before, they had ridden out for their Hallowe'en revels and thought it great fun. Now, they were leaving the only home they had ever known. It would be a hundred long years before they saw Witch Island again. Both of them sniffed, when they saw the sooty, rocky, ugly island falling away behind them.

Riding a broomstick is cold and uncomfortable at the best of times. Tonight, the wind howled around them, whipping their black rags and whistling through the holes in their pointed hats. They did not even have their red stockings to keep them warm.

Skirty Marm pressed the small radio button on her broom, which meant she could talk to Old Noshie over the roar of the wind.

"Cheer up, Nosh!"

Old Noshie pushed her radio button and said gloomily, "We'll have to live with the humans now. We'll probably get burnt."

"They haven't burned witches for hundreds of years," Skirty Marm said. "Most of them don't believe in us any more. And we've still got our magic powers."

"Yes," said Old Noshie, "but we haven't got our spellbooks."

"Oh, stop whining," Skirty Marm said crossly. "We can remember a few simple spells!"

"*You* can," sniffed Old Noshie. "You know I always have to look things up because I'm not as clever as you. I worked hard for those red stockings."

"Stop thinking about your stockings," said

Skirty Marm crossly. "We've got to decide where we're going. What about that big city where we played our Hallowe'en tricks?"

"I can't go that far," Old Noshie said in a wobbly voice. "I'm too hungry. I'd probably eat you on the way."

It took all their strength to fly now, for Mrs Abercrombie had summoned storm clouds to drive them far away from Witch Island. The bitter cold pinched their bones. Below them, they saw white-capped ocean waves, then cliffs, woods, fields and villages.

"You're good at geography," Old Noshie said. "Where are we?"

Skirty Marm frowned, trying to work it out without a map. "I think we're over a place called Hingland," she said. "They do morris dances and eat cake and drink lots of tea. Bit of a silly place by the sound of it."

"Look!" cried Old Noshie suddenly. "Over there – bats! Really juicy ones!"

The very word made their mouths water. Old Noshie was pointing to a tall stone tower with windows all round the top, and a pointed roof like a witch's hat. In the moonlight, bats swooped and fluttered around it.

Following the delicious bat smell, the two banished witches flew to the tower. They cheered up as soon as they landed in the gutter. Old Noshie put their brooms through one of the open stone windows for safe-keeping, and they settled down for a feast. They had not had a bite to eat since the ball and found the fat little bats very nourishing. When they were full, however, they realized how tired they were.

"I can't go any further," said Skirty Marm. "Let's have a sleep inside this tower."

"Right-ho," said Old Noshie.

They climbed inside and lay down on a dusty wooden floor. Skirty Marm used her hat as a pillow, and Old Noshie wrapped herself cosily in cobwebs.

"You know, Skirt," she yawned, "this isn't such a bad house. It reminds me rather of our cave." At the thought of their home (Cave 18, Stinker Street, Witch Island) she sighed. "What are we going to do for the next hundred years?"

"Well, there's one comfort about being banished," Skirty Marm said bravely. "We won't ever have to meet anyone as disgusting as Mrs Abercrombie again."

Exhausted by their horrible day, the witches fell asleep.

Little did they know that the storm clouds had blown them to someone every bit as disgusting as the queen – if not slightly worse.

3
A Bad Beginning

It was a fine, clear autumn Sunday in the little village of Tranters End. Mr Harold Snelling, the vicar of St Tranter's Church, and his poor curate, Mr Cuthbert Babbercorn, were sitting in the vestry before the service.

Mr Babbercorn was just taking a spoonful of Nasty Medicine, for his cough, when he heard a strange noise. It was a long, cackling, wicked laugh, somewhere above his head – and it gave him such a turn that he nearly dropped the medicine spoon.

"Did you hear that?" he gasped.

"Hear what?" Mr Snelling was busy eating a pork pie.

"I think," said Mr Babbercorn, "there's something cackling up in the belfry."

"Poor Cuthbert," said Mr Snelling kindly, "there's nothing up in that bell tower except a few bats. You're imagining things. I expect it's because Cousin Violet threw you downstairs again this morning."

Both men sighed deeply.

The vicar's Cousin Violet was known to everyone else as Mrs Bagg-Meanly. She kept house at the vicarage, and every soul in Tranters End was terrified of her. They quite understood why Mr Snelling hadn't dared to tell his distant cousin that he did not want a housekeeper. She had simply moved in, taking the best bedroom. She spent all Mr Snelling's money on herself and gave him such nasty food that the poor man was driven to keeping a secret supply – which she nearly always found. Only that morning she had discovered a couple of cheeses wrapped in his pyjamas and had locked them away in an iron safe in her bedroom, to eat herself.

The people of Tranters End felt very sorry for the vicar, but they were even sorrier for his young curate. If Mrs Bagg-Meanly underfed the vicar, she very nearly starved Mr Babbercorn. Though he was a good young man, she hated him and was full of plans to get rid of him. He was as thin as a stick and as pale as his own white collar, and his clothes were full of patches and darns. What little money he had of his own went on Nasty Medicine, for his cough. The village people would have loved to help him, but since Mrs Bagg-Meanly knew everything that went on, nobody dared.

"I often wonder," said Mr Snelling, "about what happened to her husband. If he ever existed."

"Perhaps she ate him," suggested Mr Babbercorn.

"If only something would happen to make her go away!" Mr Snelling sighed. "Then we'd all be free, and I could eat a decent meal at my own dining room table again. Yes, Mr Noggs?"

Mr Noggs, who was the churchwarden, had put his head round the vestry door.

"Excuse me, Vicar, Mrs Bagg-Meanly says it's time to start."

Mr Snelling and Mr Babbercorn jumped to it at once – they did not need to be told twice, with Mrs Bagg-Meanly glowering in the front pew. She was so fat, her corsets had be made specially, at a lorry factory. Her thin grey hair was squeezed into a mean, tight little bun. Her red face reminded people of a warty, bad-tempered toad.

Mr Babbercorn tried to keep very quiet and still during the service. Mrs Bagg Meanly fined them for making illegal noises in church. He owed her a small fortune for coughing, and Mr Snelling was still paying off a fart by instalments.

Halfway through the service, Mr Babbercorn heard the cackling again. Stranger still, he began to hear a tune and words – something about an old witch who was fatter than a whale. He was sure he was not imagining things.

"I won't say a word to Mrs Bagg-Meanly," he said to himself. "I'll investigate this on my own."

As soon as the service was over, while Mr Snelling was busy asking people what they were having for lunch and Mrs Bagg-Meanly was putting the collection in her handbag, Mr Babbercorn took the key to the belfry from its rusty nail and crept round to the door.

There were one hundred and eighty-six steps up to the top of the tower, and by the time he reached the top he was breathless and dizzy. His heart was thumping as he opened the door into the bell loft. What would he find?

The belfry was empty. There were the four great windows with their giddy views across the countryside. There were the two great church bells. Nothing else – unless you counted dust and cobwebs.

"And yet," murmured Mr Babbercorn, "I could have sworn—"

"BOO!" screamed a voice behind him.

The curate spun round and saw . . .

"Witches!" He fell over, in a dead faint.

When Mr Babbercorn came to, he saw two faces peering down at him curiously. One was bright green, with a luminous glow. The other was framed with a tangle of purple hair. Both looked quite friendly, but unmistakably witchy.

"Are you a policeman?" asked the one with the green face.

"No, silly," said the other. "He's a dog. Look at his collar."

Mr Babbercorn sat up. "I'm not a dog," he said. "I'm a person. But what are you? I mean, are you – can you possibly be – genuine witches?"

"Course we are," Old Noshie said scornfully. "I'm Old Noshie and this is my pal, Skirty Marm. Who are you?"

"My name is Cuthbert Babbercorn," said Mr Babbercorn.

"Ha ha ha!" shrieked the two witches. "How silly!"

Privately, Mr Babbercorn thought this was rich, coming from creatures named Old Noshie and Skirty Marm. But he was too polite to say so. "I am the curate here," he explained. "That means a sort of assistant vicar."

"Of course!" yelled Skirty Marm. "We've landed in a church! We wondered why everyone was singing."

"We had a lovely time joining in," said Old Noshie.

"I know," Mr Babbercorn said. "I heard."
How on earth was he to tell the vicar about this?
Or Mrs Bagg-Meanly?

The witches were fascinated. They had heard about churches at Human Life classes when they were Yellow-Stockings. They bombarded Mr Babbercorn with questions, but he had plenty of his own.

"What are you two doing here? Don't you have a home?"

"No," Old Noshie said sadly. "We've been banished. We sang a rude song about our stinky old queen and we went to the ball when we hadn't been invited and we had our red stockings taken away and we won't be Green-Stockings for ages."

"And we're not sorry!" shouted Skirty Marm, shaking her fist.

Since Mr Babbercorn had not understood a word of this, the witches told him the whole story. They even sang him the song about Mrs Abercrombie, though they could hardly get the words out for laughing.

"I see," Mr Babbercorn said, amazed by this strange tale. "But you still haven't said how you got all the way up to the top of a locked tower."

28

"On our broomsticks, of course," said Skirty Marm.

"What broomsticks?" asked Mr Babbercorn.

"Why, over there—" began Old Noshie.

But there were no brooms to be seen.

"Aaargh!" bellowed Skirty Marm. "You've lost our brooms, you old fool! I'll squash your nose for this!"

"I put 'em through that window," protested Old Noshie. "I know I did."

They both went quiet as they thought about it.

"I know what it is," Skirty Marm said bitterly. "It's Mrs Abercrombie. She's used the Power Hat to call back our brooms."

"No brooms!" wailed Old Noshie. "Whatever shall we do? We were going to fly off to find a new home!"

"It looks as if you'll have to stay here," said Mr Babbercorn, trying not to sound as dismayed as he felt.

"We could train up some new brooms," said Skirty Marm, "if you show us the shop that sells Witches' Requisites."

"Gosh," said Mr Babbercorn, "I don't think we have a shop like that here."

"This is a nice place," Old Noshie announced. She took Mr Babbercorn's hand. "Will you be our friend?"

"With pleasure," said Mr Babbercorn. He was a kind-hearted man and he felt sorry for these two homeless witches. "But nobody must know you are here, and you must promise to behave. No turning people into frogs, for instance."

"Frogs?" Old Noshie said scornfully. "We haven't done that since we were Yellow-Stockings. It's baby stuff."

"Well, all right," said Mr Babbercorn. "If you are going to stay, I must warn you about the Curse of Tranters End."

With a deep sigh, he told the witches about Mrs Bagg-Meanly.

"Beware of her," he said. "She is wicked and mean and she will hate any friend of mine."

"We'll try very hard to be good," promised Skirty Marm. "It might be difficult at first, because we've never done it before. But we'll soon get the hang of it."

Mr Babbercorn got up from the floor and dusted himself down. "I must go," he said, glancing at his watch. "If I'm one second late for lunch, Mrs Bagg-Meanly puts it on the compost heap. I say – what will you two do about food?"

"We eat the bats," said Old Noshie. She plucked one out of her sleeve and ate it in a single gulp.

Mr Babbercorn wished he could fancy a bat. He was sure it would be more nourishing than Mrs Bagg-Meanly's cabbage pie.

"Goodbye, then," he said. "I'll come and see you tomorrow."

"What a nice human," said Old Noshie when he had gone. "And I'm looking forward to fixing up our new home."

"A few more cobwebs, a couple more mouldy patches, a touch of dry rot," said Skirty Marm happily, "and it could really look quite tasteful."

Old Noshie took a slurp of rainwater out of the gutter. "If only we had our spellbooks," she said.

"Pooh," Skirty Marm said, "stop going on about those."

"But, Skirt, how can we train up new broomsticks without them? I don't fancy being stuck here without a broom."

"I know the training spell by heart," said Skirty Marm. "I won a medal for broom-

31

training at school, don't forget. We'll show Mrs A. she can't beat us!"

Remembering that their new friend had asked them to stay out of sight, the witches waited until the moon rose and the village was cloaked in darkness. Then they trotted down the one hundred and eighty-six belfry steps and into the high street. It was cold and drizzly and – luckily for the witches – not another soul was awake. At first, they walked about on tiptoe and were very, very good, for they had always wanted to get a close look at the way humans lived.

"What funny little birds," remarked Skirty Marm, looking at the ducks on the pond. "I wonder if they're nice to eat? We might get tired of bats."

Old Noshie was admiring a cluster of thatched cottages. "Why have those houses got hair?"

"Silly, that's not hair," said Skirty Marm. "That's their little hats, to keep off the rain."

They both sniggered, thinking the humans were very silly for not liking a drop of rain.

"Wow!" Skirty Marm said suddenly. "Look at this!"

She dragged her friend over to the window of

the Post Office and General Shop, and the two witches were so thrilled with what they saw there that they were quiet for nearly five minutes.

Crammed into the window were garden rakes, jars of sweets, aprons, babies' dresses, wellington boots, knitting wool, flower seeds and coloured postcards. Most interestingly of all, right at the back were two long BROOMS.

"Just what we need," whispered Skirty Marm. "We must take them at once and start work."

"Shouldn't we ask our new friend first?" Old

Noshie remembered Mr Babbercorn. "He said we had to behave."

"We'll ask him after we've nicked them," said Skirty Marm firmly.

She mumbled a spell and the post office window melted into mist. The two witches simply walked in, helped themselves to the brooms and hurried back to their belfry.

"Beautiful," said Skirty Marm when they were safely back in their new home. "Look at the workmanship. You don't get brooms like this on Witch Island."

"I nicked something else, too," Old Noshie said proudly. From under her rags, she pulled out a picture-postcard of the church. "Let's send it to Mrs A.!"

"Heeheehee!" cackled Skirty Marm. "I'd like to see her face when she gets it, the mean old slug!"

They wrote on the back of the card in Old Noshie's blood, which was dark green.

To old roten egg sumtimes known as Mrs Abercrombie Cave 1 Witch Island. Dere roten egg we R having a luvly time this is a piktur of our howse the wether is grate so POOH to you luv Old Noshie and Skirty Marm.

When they had stopped laughing, they sent this elegant message off to Witch Island, using a basic posting spell. Then it was time to tackle the far harder task of training their new broomsticks. Breaking in a broom is never easy. The witches did not have their spellbooks, and Skirty Marm's memory was not as good as she liked to pretend.

At first, they made all kinds of mistakes. Old Noshie changed the brooms into bicycles, which took ages to put right. Skirty Marm accidentally summoned a genie, who was very cross about being disturbed for nothing. Finally, after hours of wailing, quarrelling and biffing each other's noses, they managed to get the brooms to obey a few simple commands.

"Come on, let's go and find somewhere to practise," said Skirty Marm.

The two witches ran down the one hundred and eighty-six steps just as the sun was rising. In their excitement they had forgotten their promise to Mr Babbercorn, to stay out of sight.

4

Worse

In the high street, the sun had risen on a scene of panic. A crowd of people, all very excited, had gathered round the post office. Mrs Tucker, the postmistress, was sipping tea and telling her story to Constable Bloater, the local policeman.

". . . I came downstairs and there was my window. Or rather, there it wasn't . . ."

"Must've been a whole gang of them," said PC Bloater. "But what did they do with the broken glass? A whole window can't have vanished into thin air!"

Mr Snelling and Mr Babbercorn, who had heard the commotion, came running over from the vicarage.

"What's going on?" panted the vicar.

"There's been a robbery, that's what," said Mrs Tucker crossly.

"Dear, dear," said Mr Snelling, "what did they take?"

"That's the funny thing," said PC Bloater. "If you don't count the window, nothing but a postcard and two garden brooms."

"The old-fashioned sort," said Mrs Tucker, "like witches have in stories—"

"Oh, no!" squeaked Mr Babbercorn. At once, he guessed who was responsible.

Everyone turned to stare at him. Fortunately for the witches, however, they were distracted by the sound of a door slamming at the vicarage. The ground began to shake. A mighty voice boomed, "And *what*, may I ask, is the meaning of *this*?"

At once, everyone – even the ducks in the pond – fell silent. Up the street and through the little crowd stomped the enormous, terrible figure of Mrs Bagg-Meanly.

She wore a purple dressing gown, which exactly matched the colour of her toad-like face. Her thin, straggly hair was covered with a purple net. As it was early morning, she hadn't shaved and bristly grey hairs sprouted around her mouth.

"There . . . there's been a robbery, Cousin

Violet," faltered Mr Snelling.

"Who done it?" shouted Mrs Bagg-Meanly. "Nobody moves till I find out!"

"I'm taking care of things here," said PC Bloater weakly.

Mrs Bagg-Meanly's fist shot out. She knocked PC Bloater's helmet onto the ground. "Just because you wear a helmet, Bill Bloater, it don't make you Sherlock Holmes! I'll tell you what's going on. It's a plot, to upset my nerves. You'll all be sorry for this!"

Everyone trembled. They were sorry already.

It was at this moment that Mr Babbercorn happened to glance up at the church tower. What he saw made his heart sink. Two ragged black figures on broomsticks were whizzing round and round the steeple. In a moment, the whole village would know about the witches – and then what would happen to them?

Suddenly there was a resounding crash of breaking glass, as if a window had smashed in every single house in the village at the same time.

As they found out afterwards, this was exactly what had happened. Through each smashed window flew a stream of brooms, mops and brushes. The gaping villagers watched in stunned silence as their domestic implements glided gracefully down the high street.

PC Bloater was slightly grazed by his own lavatory brush, as it whistled past his ear. Eighteen mops got tangled in the telephone wires, which put the village telephones out of order for a week.

Mrs Bagg-Meanly squeaked, "My best big scrubbing-brush!" and fainted on top of Mr Babbercorn.

The brushes, mops and brooms turned the corner in neat formation and shot off in the direction of the motorway. They were never seen again and nobody ever found out what became of them.

There was a long silence, then Mr Snelling cleared his throat and said, "Did you all see that too?"

Immediately, realizing they had not gone mad, everyone began talking at once. What on earth had made their brooms and brushes fly away? Was it something to do with the ozone layer? Was it because Tranters End had been built on a mammoth's burial ground? Was it awesome science or fearsome magic?

"It was magic!" quavered Mrs Bagg-Meanly.

"Terrible magic!" She looked – very unusually – frightened. "Don't let it come near me!"

Then a little colour crept into her pale face. In her usual voice, she shouted, "I'm lying on something bony! Take it away!" From underneath her, Mr Snelling and PC Bloater pulled out the squashed, gasping figure of Mr Babbercorn.

"I might have known it was you, you nasty young man," grumbled Mrs Bagg-Meanly. "Don't you ever get underneath me again. It was like lying on a toast rack."

"Sorry," croaked Mr Babbercorn feebly.

The horrible housekeeper lumbered to her size eleven feet.

"I'm going for a lie-down till lunch," she announced, "so this village had better be quiet! If I'm disturbed . . ."

She did not need to finish the sentence. Her face looked so menacing that a deathly silence fell instantly. You could almost hear the beetles rustling in the grass. The size eleven feet went stomp-stomp-stomp back to the vicarage.

Mr Babbercorn wondered why Mrs Bagg-Meanly had looked so frightened – he hadn't expected her to believe in magic. He was not in the mood to wonder for long, however – there were far more urgent things on his mind. He was very much afraid that Old Noshie and Skirty Marm had more tricks up their ragged sleeves.

Mr Babbercorn was right – his witch troubles had only just begun. A little while earlier, Old Noshie and Skirty Marm had started training their new brooms in earnest. The two witches had found a deserted field where they hoped they could soon begin proper flying. Skirty Marm had some difficulty remembering all the right commands for novice brooms. Waking up every broom, mop and brush in the village had been her fault. Both the witches howled and screamed with laughter when they saw the procession of cleaning things hurtling down the street.

"You old silly," sniggered Old Noshie. "They'll all have to buy new ones now."

"Pooh," said Skirty Marm proudly. "These humans do far too much cleaning anyway. And I've remembered the proper spell now. Don't interrupt."

She mumbled a few words, and both witches shrieked with delight. The two brooms twitched, rose gently into the air, flew once

41

round the field, then returned to be mounted.

"Good as gold," said Old Noshie, giving her broom a pat.

"Very comfy," said Skirty Marm as she mounted. "Not even Purple-Stockings have brooms as smart as these!"

There was a lot of wobbling and falling off at first, but before long the new broomsticks were behaving beautifully. That was when Old Noshie and Skirty Marm went whizzing round the steeple – they had quite forgotten their promise to stay out of sight.

"Whee! Look at me!" shouted Skirty Marm. She did a loop-the-loop, and both witches cackled when her hat fell off into a tree.

Old Noshie invented a brilliant new game. She flew high into the air and dropped her bright blue wig, and the witches had to catch it before it hit the ground. It was great fun. They were both in high spirits, and Skirty Marm was feeling particularly cocky.

"Look down there," she said, pointing to the crowd around the post office. "It's our friend, Mr B.! Shall we wave?"

"Better not. We promised to stay out of sight," said Old Noshie, feeling very virtuous.

"Let's go and have a good snoop around his house instead."

"Good idea," said Skirty Marm, pointing her broom towards the vicarage roof.

The vicarage, home of Mr Snelling, Mr Babbercorn and Mrs Bagg-Meanly, was a large, red-brick house, next to the church. The two witches hovered round the windows on their broomsticks, peeping in at all the rooms and enjoying themselves very much.

The first room they looked into was Mrs Bagg-Meanly's bedroom. It had a soft pink carpet, two cosy armchairs and a big iron safe in one corner. There was also a treacle tart on the windowsill. The witches had never seen a treacle tart before. They ate it and decided it was delicious.

The next window belonged to Mr Snelling's bedroom. This was not nearly so comfortable, but Old Noshie and Skirty Marm found several very interesting things which I shall come to later.

Last of all, they flew up to the attics and found the miserable little garret where Mr Babbercorn slept. The windows were broken. The floor was bare and full of splinters. The bed looked as hard as cement. And on the table stood a large brown bottle of . . .

"Hooray! Nasty Medicine!" cried Skirty Marm, snatching it greedily.

"Give us a swig, you old meanie!" roared Old Noshie, nearly toppling off her broom.

"No, I've got a better idea," said Skirty Marm. "Let's take it back to our tower and have a party. We can celebrate finding our new brooms."

Off the witches went, at the very moment Mr Babbercorn was being dragged out from under Mrs Bagg-Meanly. Shaken by the experience and worried that it would bring on his cough, he hurried up to his bedroom to take some Nasty Medicine.

"It's a mercy Mrs Bagg-Meanly didn't see the witches," he said to himself.

He looked on the table for his bottle of Nasty Medicine.

"Gone!" he cried. "Who would be wicked enough to steal my Nasty Medicine? Don't they know how DANGEROUS and STUPID it is to drink someone else's Nasty Medicine?"

Meanwhile, in the belfry, Old Noshie and Skirty Marm had finished the bottle. As I have said before, it is extremely DANGEROUS for humans to touch someone else's medicine. The witches were not humans, however, and all it did was make them shockingly tipsy.

"Let's have some fun, Nosh!" said Skirty Marm.

"What shall we do?" asked Old Noshie.

As usual, Skirty Marm was full of ideas. "Let's have a game of Vests-in-the-Rain."

Vests-in-the-Rain was a disgusting game, very popular among the Red-Stockings on Witch Island. You had to fly your broomstick over a washing line and spit at the washing below. If you hit an item of underwear, you got ten points.

There was a lot of underwear hanging out in Tranters End on this brisk, breezy day. Skirty Marm scored two hundred and eighty points. Old Noshie, who was not such a good shot, scored one hundred and sixty.

"I'm running out of dribble," she said eventually. "What shall we do now?"

"Let's have a sit-down on the vicar's roof," said Skirty Marm, "and shout rude things."

"Brilliant!" cried Old Noshie.

They flew over to the vicarage and perched comfortably on the sloping roof with their feet in the gutter. They did not have long to wait for the fun to begin.

Below them, they heard the booming voice of Mrs Bagg-Meanly.

"Harold Snelling! Have you been snooping in my bedroom?"

"Me, Cousin Violet?" squeaked the Vicar. "Never!"

"Then where," said Mrs Bagg-Meanly, "is my treacle tart?"

"I don't know, Cousin Violet. Honestly."

Up on the roof, the witches burst into giggles.

"I've made up one of my songs," said Skirty Marm. At the top of her voice, she began to chant:

> "He did not eat your treacle tart,
> He did not eat your pie,
> He does not need to steal your grub
> And here's the reason why."

"Where's that voice coming from?" yelled Mrs Bagg-Meanly. "Who's singing? Stop it, this instant, or I'll call the police!"

But the rude voice on the roof went on:

> "I had a look inside his room
> And found it full of eats;
> He has a row of hollow books,
> And fills them up with sweets!"

"Oh, they're *hollow*, are they?" said Mrs Bagg-Meanly menacingly. "I might have guessed."

"Please, Cousin Violet," begged poor Mr Snelling, "it won't happen again!"

On went the voice:

"What a funny man he is,
To fill the sink with bread!
There's jam tarts in his pillowcase
And biscuits in his bed!"

"I'd better take a look!" trumpeted Mrs Bagg-Meanly. "Stand aside, Harold!"

On the roof, Old Noshie said, "My turn!" She shouted:

"Behind a picture of his aunt,
There is some marzipan;
I think you'd better punish him –
He's such a greedy man!"

"Punish him?" said Mrs Bagg-Meanly. "I certainly will!"

The witches heard several thumps and crashes and muffled cries of "Ow!"

How could they? thought Mr Babbercorn, who had of course been listening. "Poor Mr Snelling – he's been hoarding that secret food for weeks!" And he burst into a fit of coughing.

The last thing the witches heard, as they wobbled back to their belfry, was Mrs Bagg-Meanly shouting, "Don't you corf at me, young man! I will not have corfing!" Followed by more thumps and crashes.

The witches were not sorry for the trouble they had caused. They were feeling very tired now and all they wanted to do was sleep.

Three hours later, when Mr Babbercorn climbed the one hundred and eighty-six steps up to the belfry and opened the door, a very vulgar scene met his eyes.

Old Noshie and Skirty Marm lay snoring on the floor with their hats over their eyes. The two stolen brooms lay in one corner with the empty bottle of Nasty Medicine between them.

"Witches," said Mr Babbercorn sternly, "wake up at once!"

Old Noshie and Skirty Marm took their hats off their faces and groaned.

"I feel terrible!" wailed Skirty Marm. "I'll never touch another drop as long as I live!"

"Hello, Mr B.," said Old Noshie. "Have you come to cheer us up?"

"Certainly not!" said Mr Babbercorn. "I've been squashed flat, Mr Snelling has had his secret food taken away, the whole village is in an uproar – and it's all your fault!"

49

"Well, of all the cheek," Old Noshie said huffily. "What have *we* done?"

"You stole two brooms," Mr Babbercorn said. "You flew about on them in broad daylight. You broke windows all over Tranters End and made all the mops and brushes escape. You sang a dreadful song, which got the vicar into trouble with Mrs Bagg-Meanly. You zoomed about spitting on people's washing – oh, yes, you did. I saw you, and it's a miracle nobody else did. Worst of all, you stole my Nasty Medicine – even though drinking someone else's medicine is extremely WICKED and DANGEROUS. Oh, witches! How could you be so naughty?"

The witches hung their heads.

"I want to be your friend," said Mr Babbercorn, "but I don't see how I can be if you're going to behave like this."

"We didn't mean to be naughty," mumbled Skirty Marm. "We were only having a bit of fun."

"We got you into trouble when we promised to be good!" cried Old Noshie, bursting into tears. And they both began to wail and sob and howl until Mr Babbercorn was afraid someone would hear.

"Be quiet!" he hissed. "I'll forgive you, if you swear you'll give up your bad, witchy ways and try hard to be good."

"We will!" they cried. "We'll try ever so hard! Please don't stop being our friend!"

Mr Babbercorn took out his handkerchief and blew his nose. He was very touched by the witches' repentance. "We'll say no more about it then. We'll start all over again. Goodbye, witches." He hurried away down the one hundred and eighty-six steps.

Old Noshie and Skirty Marm were sadder and wiser witches now.

"Noshie," said Skirty Marm in a solemn voice, "from tomorrow we'll be so good our new friend will hardly recognize us."

5

Shrinking Violet

Next morning, the witches woke before dawn and remembered this was the first day of their new life of Virtue. They were rather depressed.

"Blimey," complained Skirty Marm, "how do you go about being good? Can you remember anything about being good in our spellbooks, Nosh?"

"Nope," said Old Noshie. "All they said was how to be bad. That was the whole point."

They thought very hard and decided to start by mixing Mr Babbercorn some new Nasty Medicine for his cough. This was tricky without their spellbooks, but Skirty Marm was sure she remembered the recipe. As the sun rose, they flew over the fields collecting herbs and berries. Then they boiled them up in rainwater – using Old Noshie's hat as a saucepan – and poured the mixture into Mr Babbercorn's medicine bottle.

"Skirt," said Old Noshie in a worried voice, "I don't remember it being pink . . . Are you sure you've got it right?"

Skirty Marm was not very sure, but said crossly, "Of course it's right, you old fool. Anyway, it's prettier than the old stuff. I bet he'll be pleased."

After checking there was nobody about, the two witches flew over to the vicarage and left the bottle on Mr Babbercorn's windowsill. They waited in a mulberry tree nearby for him to find it.

"I've thought of something else," said Old

Noshie. "Is a witch cough the same as a human cough?"

"All right, smelly!" shouted Skirty Marm. "Make it yourself if you're so clever!"

"Sorry," mumbled Old Noshie.

"Shhh!" whispered Skirty Marm. "Here he comes!"

But it was not Mr Babbercorn. Mrs Bagg-Meanly stomped into the curate's bedroom to polish the floor, hoping he would slip and break something. To the horror of the witches, she walked straight over to the bottle of Nasty Medicine. The autumn sun, suddenly bursting through the clouds, lit it up like a pink jewel.

"Hmmm," said Mrs Bagg-Meanly, "this isn't the stuff the little beast usually takes!" She took out the cork and sniffed it suspiciously. "Delicious! Far too good for the likes of him!"

And she swigged the whole lot, in one big gulp.

"Greedy pig!" wailed Skirty Marm, "Now we'll have to make some more!"

"Skirt!" gasped Old Noshie. "Look!"

A strange expression was creeping over Mrs Bagg-Meanly's face – as well it might, for something awful was happening to her.

"Help! Police!" she screamed. "I'm SHRINKING!"

And so she was. Her mighty voice was shrinking, too, until it was hardly more than a mouse's squeak.

"Told you it was the wrong potion," Old Noshie whispered. "What a good thing Mr B. didn't drink it."

Mrs Bagg-Meanly's little head vanished beneath the edge of the table, and the two witches laughed so hard they had to clutch their brooms to stop themselves falling out of the tree.

"Let's go and take a look at her," said Skirty Marm.

They squeezed themselves and their broom sticks through Mr Babbercorn's broken bedroom window. Mrs Bagg-Meanly was now about the size of a teacup. The witches laughed even harder and this made Mrs Bagg-Meanly very angry.

She shook her tiny fist at them. "If you two are responsible for this, you put me right at once!"

"Heeheehee!" tittered Skirty Marm. "Impossible!"

"We don't know how!" sniggered Old Noshie.

This was quite true. The antidote to the spell was in the Red-Stocking Spellbook – which, of course, they didn't have.

"You'll suffer for this. I have connections," raged Mrs Bagg-Meanly. "Nobody does magic on me and gets away with it!"

She bit Old Noshie's toe.

"Ow!" complained Old Noshie. "She's ever so vicious, Skirt. Put her in the medicine bottle and cork her up tight."

"Good idea," said Skirty Marm.

Mrs Bagg-Meanly kicked and screamed, but to no avail. She was rammed down the neck of the bottle and corked up in her glass prison.

"Skirt," Old Noshie said uneasily, "will Mr Babbercorn be pleased about this?"

"Deary me," said Skirty Marm, "he ought to be. But he's such a funny little thing – he might say we've been naughty."

"And I've thought of something else." Old Noshie sounded scared. "Suppose the spell wears off? Think what she'll do to him when she grows again!"

They stared at each other, dismayed. What had they done? And at that very moment, they heard Mr Babbercorn coming up the stairs. The cowardly witches did not dare to face him. They jumped on their brooms and fled back to the belfry.

When Mr Babbercorn entered his bedroom, the fateful bottle was the first thing he saw.

"I do believe those witches have mixed me some new medicine!" he said. "How kind!"

But when he picked up the bottle, he got one of the worst shocks of his life.

"It can't be!" he gasped. "I must be seeing things!"

Inside the bottle, tiny Mrs Bagg-Meanly was stamping her little feet. Mr Babbercorn looked out of the window – just in time to glimpse a guilty green face in the belfry.

Very carefully, he took out the cork.

"Wait till I grow again!" shrilled the little voice. "You'll be sorry you was ever born!"

"I'm afraid there's nothing I can do," Mr Babbercorn said, quite kindly. "There's been a dreadful mistake."

He popped the cork back, wondering what to do.

"I'll tell the vicar," he decided. "He's such a sensible man."

Holding the bottle very carefully, he went

down to Mr Snelling's study.

"Excuse me, Vicar," he said. "I have to speak to you urgently. It's about Mrs Bagg-Meanly."

"Keep your voice down!" hissed Mr Snelling. "She'll hear you!"

"She won't," said Mr Babbercorn. "Something has happened to her. Something terrible."

Mr Snelling's face became bright with hope. "Has she gone to live with her sister?"

Mr Babbercorn said, "I'm holding her in my hand."

Amazed, Mr Snelling stared into the bottle and saw Mrs Bagg-Meanly's toad-like mouth opening and shutting.

"Good gracious," he said, "it's Cousin Violet!"

"I can't quite explain how," said Mr Babbercorn, "but a spell has been cast on her. I was hoping you'd know what to do."

"DO?" shouted the vicar. "Are you mad? She's shut in a bottle and she can't get out! Oh, joy! Oh, rapture!"

He did a little dance and kissed Mr Babbercorn on the nose.

"This is the happiest day of my life! Tell you what, Cuthbert, we'll have a feast of my secret food to celebrate. And Cousin Violet can watch us eat it!"

"But Vicar . . ." began Mr Babbercorn. "What if she grows back again?"

"Nonsense!" sang Mr Snelling. "Don't be such a wet blanket!"

He crouched down and stuck his tongue out at the bottle. Mrs Bagg-Meanly danced with fury, but there was nothing she could do.

"Cuthbert," Mr Snelling said briskly, "run round to Mrs Noggs and tell her we can't come to the jumble sale meeting. I'll get the lunch."

Mr Babbercorn ran out at once. He did not, however, go to Mrs Noggs. Up the one hundred and eighty-six steps to the belfry he pelted, and found Old Noshie and Skirty Marm hiding their guilty faces in their hats.

"I want an explanation!" he said sternly.

"Don't be cross," moaned Old Noshie. "It was a mistake!"

"I'm sure you meant well," said Mr Babbercorn, "and I'll admit I am tempted to leave her in the bottle. But you can't go round casting spells on people. You must put it right at once."

"We can't remember how," Skirty Marm said

forlornly. "But we have remembered something." She did not dare to look Mr Babbercorn in the eye. "The . . . the spell wears off at sunset."

"No!" groaned Mr Babbercorn. "Oh, witches, witches, what shall I do? No, don't start crying! You've got to think of a way to put this ghastly mess right."

"Forgive us!" begged the weeping witches.

"Yes, yes – just do what you can." And Mr Babbercorn rushed back to the vicarage.

He found Mr Snelling spreading his secret food across the dining room table. The vicar was in a festive mood – he was singing, and he had tied one of Mrs Bagg-Meanly's elastic stockings in a bow round his bald head.

"Vicar," began Mr Babbercorn, "I'm afraid I've got some rather worrying—"

"Honestly, Cuthbert," said Mr Snelling, "what an old fusspot you are! Sit down and eat, before these lovely chips go cold."

"But we can't—"

"Have a smartie." The vicar pushed his curate into a chair and made a hideous face at the bottle.

Inside it, the rage of the teeny Mrs Bagg-

Meanly was a terrible thing to behold.

Sunset! thought Mr Babbercorn. It's November and it'll be dark in no time! Suppose the witches can't do anything?

He looked at the delicious food on his plate. There were chips, beefburgers, pork pies, chocolate cakes and loads of sweets. Mr Babbercorn was very hungry and ate every crumb. But the feast was quite spoiled by the sight of the sun sinking slowly outside the dining-room window.

Mr Snelling ate and ate, until the red sun was just on the point of dipping into the horizon.

"Lovely," he declared, wiping chocolate off his mouth. "Best meal I ever had."

Mr Babbercorn cleared up the crumbs and took the dirty plates to the kitchen. Where, oh where were Old Noshie and Skirty Marm when he needed them? He washed the dishes quickly and hurried back to the dining room.

The vicar had let Mrs Bagg-Meanly out of the bottle and was making her jump over his finger while she scampered furiously across the table.

"You'll be sorry for this, Harold Snelling!" she squeaked in her tiny voice.

"Silly old Cousin Violet!" giggled Mr Snelling. "What can you do to me?"

"I'll tread on your glasses . . . I'll burst your
hot-water bottle . . . I'll bite your ears until you
beg for mercy—"

"Back in your bottle, Cousin Violet, dear!"
sang Mr Snelling.

But at that moment, the sun sank below the
horizon. Mr Babbercorn's spirits sank with it.
Too late!

"Aaarrgh!" screamed the vicar.

Mrs Bagg-Meanly was grinning now, for she
was growing larger every second. First, she was
the size of the medicine bottle, then she was the
size of a chair, and in no time she was her old

self again – standing on the table with her arms folded.

"Well, well, well," she said, "what a LOVELY day you've had, Harold."

"Cousin Violet . . ." It was the vicar's turn to squeak now. "I can explain—"

"And YOU!" she roared at Mr Babbercorn. "You little squirt! You horrible, sneaking little runt! When I've finished with you, you won't have a whole bone left! I'll send you back to the bishop in an envelope!"

Mr Babbercorn trembled, but suddenly saw two witchy faces peeping over the windowsill. He heard two voices muttering a spell. He held his breath.

A look of bewilderment dawned on Mrs Bagg-Meanly's face. "Where am I?" she croaked. "What am I doing standing on the table? Help me down . . . I've come over all queer . . . I don't remember a thing . . ."

She was pale green and shaking. The vicar and Mr Babbercorn helped her down from the table, and she did not even try to hit them. Groaning softly, she tottered away to her bedroom.

For several minutes, Mr Snelling and Mr Babbercorn stood in dazed silence.

"She's . . . she's lost her memory," Mr Babbercorn said. "We're safe."

He made a pot of tea with two teabags left over from the feast, and they sat down to recover from their fright.

"It was a lovely day," sighed Mr Snelling presently. "And what a lucky escape we had – I was just about to mix a trifle in her best hat!"

Very quietly, they laughed.

The only reminder of that strange afternoon was a row of tiny footprints in the butter.

6

Mr Babbercorn's Birthday

After the shrinking incident, the rest of November passed peacefully in Tranters End. Old Noshie and Skirty Marm worked hard at being good – even when Mr Babbercorn insisted that being good meant no more magic.

"But some of our spells are very kind!" argued Skirty Marm.

"If you want to live in this village," Mr Babbercorn said firmly, "you have to behave like humans. And that means no spells at all. Even kind ones. No more swooping about on your brooms in broad daylight. And definitely no more games of Vests-in-the-Rain."

"Oh, well," said Old Noshie, "we'll do our best. We don't want to get banished again."

There was one bad incident when they turned the parrot on Mrs Tucker's best hat into a vulture. On the whole, however, the two witches were doing well. They began to settle into a routine, staying in their belfry when it was light and only flying out on their brooms when darkness fell.

Skirty Marm sometimes moaned that being good was boring, but she wanted to stay in Tranters End. There were lots of things about the village that she liked very much – for instance, when the great church bells rang on Sunday mornings. Humans would have found the noise in the belfry unbearable, but the witches loved the din and had great fun riding on the bells as they rocked to and fro.

Best of all, they had a real friend. Mr Babbercorn climbed the one hundred and eighty-six steps nearly every day to drink warm rainwater with the witches and listen to their tales of Witch Island. He had grown very fond of Old Noshie and Skirty Marm and often thought how lonely he would feel without them.

One morning, in early December, when the woods and fields were white with the first snow, Old Noshie said to Skirty Marm, "Skirt, I wish we had some money. Today is Mr Babbercorn's birthday. Wouldn't it be nice to give him a present?"

"Oh yes, let's," said Skirty Marm. "Poor thing – he gets weedier every day. Even his delicious Nasty Medicine doesn't seem to do him any good. That stinky Mrs Bagg-Meanly is starving him, when he should be having a lovely tea party."

The curate had told them all about human birthdays, and they were very sorry they could not give him a cake with candles on – they thought this sounded wonderful. Birthdays were never noticed on Witch Island, unless a witch was moving into new stockings. Even then, nobody had much fun.

"Maybe we could nick something?" suggested Old Noshie.

Skirty Marm shook her head. "He'd only get cross, and we don't want that. But I've had a brilliant idea!"

While the witches were planning his birthday, Mr Babbercorn was chopping wood in the vicarage garden, blowing on his fingers to stop them turning blue with cold. He was quite alone. Mrs Bagg-Meanly had gone shopping for the day, and Mr Snelling had a jumble sale meeting.

Mrs Bagg-Meanly had been careful to lock up every crumb of food, and Mr Babbercorn had not had a bite to eat for two days. He was so hungry he had even tried eating a used teabag he had fished out of the dustbin.

"I don't think I've ever been so miserable," he said to himself. "Never mind, when I've finished here I'll go and call on the witches. They always cheer me up."

He raised the axe to make another chop, and gasped, "Ow!"

Something extremely peculiar was happening. The ground fell away under his feet, the axe dropped from his hand, and he found himself floating high in the air with his chin resting on the Vicar's bedroom windowsill.

"Goodness," he exclaimed, "I appear to be – flying!"

A gust of wind blew him over the chimney in a perfect somersault. He flew out over the high street like a kite.

Below him, Mrs Tucker and Mrs Noggs were sweeping their garden paths.

"Well I never," remarked Mrs Tucker, "there goes Mr Babbercorn!"

"Poor young dear," said Mrs Noggs from the other side of the fence. "I always said he was an angel."

"What shall I do?" wondered Mr Babbercorn. "Perhaps I should ask Mrs Noggs to call the fire brigade. How long will I be stuck up here?"

His question was answered by another gust of wind. A moment later, he was sitting on the floor of the belfry with his glasses hanging off one ear.

"Hahahaha!" shrieked Old Noshie and Skirty Marm.

"I might have known you two would be at the bottom of this," said Mr Babbercorn, trying to look strict. "What are you up to?"

"Happy birthday to you!" bawled the witches. "Happy birthday to you, happy birthday DEAR CUTHBERT, happy birthday to you!"

"It's my birthday!" cried Mr Babbercorn. "I quite forgot!"

"And we've got a present for you," said Skirty Marm. "You're going to have a holiday."

"Now that you can fly," Old Noshie said, "we're going to take you somewhere lovely – only you mustn't ask where because it's a surprise."

"I don't suppose it would matter," Mr Babbercorn said thoughtfully, "just for one day.

Why not? I haven't had a holiday for years. I'm sure it would do me good."

"Hurrah, that's settled then!" crowed Skirty Marm. "Follow us!"

She grabbed Mr Babbercorn's hand, and he was slightly alarmed to find himself being pulled out of the window. They came out above thick clouds, soaking wet and very cold. Clutching the back of Old Noshie's broomstick, the curate flew higher and higher, faster and faster.

After a while, he noticed he was getting warmer. At first, he thought this must be because of the effort of holding onto the broom, but presently he became so hot that he took off his jacket, then his scarf, then his pullover. Though he had no clue where he was, he realized how fast they were going when they overtook an aeroplane. He just had time to glimpse the astonished face of the pilot, before they left it far behind.

Suddenly the clouds melted away and he was gazing down at a deep blue sea, winking like a sheet of sapphire in the blazing sun.

"We're here!" cried Old Noshie.

The warm air rushed around him, and Mr Babbercorn landed on something beautifully

soft. He opened his eyes and was speechless with delight. They were on a long, white beach with waves lapping gently at the sand, tall palm trees and scented groves of fruit.

While he gazed around, the witches watched him anxiously.

"Well?" asked Skirty Marm. "Do you . . . do you like it?"

"Oh, witches, it's perfect!" said Mr Babbercorn. "It's the best birthday present I ever had!"

Old Noshie blushed dark green with pleasure, and Skirty Marm's purple hair crackled with pride. They had never given anyone a present before (there was no such thing on Witch Island) and they liked the feeling extremely.

"Let's have lunch," said Old Noshie.

Flying from tree to tree on their broomsticks, the two witches gathered piles of coconuts, pineapples, oranges, dates and bananas. They all ate until they were full and sticky with juices.

Mr Babbercorn could hardly believe his luck. Only that morning he had been slaving in the vicarage garden. Now here he was, sunbathing on a desert island.

Bless these witches, he thought. How glad I am that they came to Tranters End.

All that long afternoon they played games in the sand, paddled in the sea, or simply lay basking in the shimmering heat. They made a sandcastle using the witches' hats as buckets. Noshie and Skirty taught Mr Babbercorn to play Witch Football, with an invisible ball, and magicked up a rather mouldy-tasting birthday cake.

At last, when the tropical sun was turning red, Mr Babbercorn sighed and said, "I'm afraid it's time we were getting back." He could not help looking sad as he fastened on his curate's collar.

They all sat quietly, thinking of the wintry village, the icy vicarage and wicked Mrs Bagg-Meanly.

"We won't let you go back!" blurted Skirty Marm. "We'll stay here for ever!"

"We can build a nice little house in a tree," Old Noshie said comfortably. "Won't that be fun?"

Mr Babbercorn shook his head. "I'm sorry, witches. You may stay here, but I must go home."

"Why?" asked Skirty Marm. "You don't like it."

"Humans have to do lots of things they don't

like," Mr Babbercorn explained. "I am the curate at Tranters End – which means the people need me, not to mention poor Mr Snelling. It would be awfully mean of me to leave him alone."

"Deary me," said Old Noshie in a disappointed voice, "how horrid it is, being good."

Skirty Marm had a worrying thought. "I say – you do want us to come back with you, don't you?"

Mr Babbercorn laughed. "Of course. You're my best friends."

The witches beamed, feeling very honoured.

"We'll come home then," she announced. "I would have missed our tower, anyway."

"Hmph," muttered Old Noshie crossly. She had been looking forward to setting up house in a tree.

"I'll tell you a human saying," said Mr Babbercorn. "It goes like this: *East, West, Home's Best*. Even when it's not perfect, or even very nice, it's still home."

Old Noshie brightened. She could never stay in a bad mood for long. "It won't be so bad, if we take some fruit back with us."

The two witches filled their hats with fruit, and Mr Babbercorn tucked the biggest pineapple he could find inside his jacket as a present for the vicar. When darkness began to fall across that lovely island, they all flew home.

More snow had fallen during the afternoon, and the air was crisp with frost. By the light of the moon, holly berries glowed scarlet among their spiked green leaves.

Mr Babbercorn yawned when the three of them landed in the belfry.

"I can't thank you enough for this gorgeous day," he said. "I feel ten years younger!"

"I wish we could do it every day," Old Noshie said sadly.

"Cheer up, Noshie!" said Mr Babbercorn. "Think what fun you'll have in all this snow. You've never seen proper, thick snow before. Tomorrow, I'll tell you how to make a toboggan."

Old Noshie and Skirty Marm thought a toboggan sounded brilliant, and when Mr Babbercorn went away down the one hundred and eighty-six steps he left two very contented witches behind him.

"Didn't he look happy, Skirt?" mused Old

Noshie as she mulled over the glories of the day. "Wasn't it great, to see him smile and play?"

"Tell you what, Nosh," said Skirty Marm, "I'm beginning to see the point of this being good lark. I think it has something to do with the lovely feeling you get when you make a nice person happy. If this is being good, I like it!"

The next morning, Mr Babbercorn and Mr Snelling sat at breakfast in the kitchen while Mrs Bagg-Meanly ate a private (and much bigger) breakfast in the dining room. Mr Snelling counted out the ten cornflakes they were each allowed and rustled his newspaper.

"Here's a funny story," he said. "Listen to this: 'I Saw Flying Parson Claims Airline Pilot.' What next, eh?" He glanced up at Mr Babbercorn. "Goodness, Cuthbert, how well you look. If it wasn't December, I'd say you had a suntan!"

Mr Babbercorn whispered, "I've got a pineapple for you."

"A pineapple!" gasped Mr Snelling. "Where did you get a pineapple?"

"Ask no questions," said Mr Babbercorn with a meaningful wink, "and you'll be told no lies."

7

The Divine Floradora

Christmas was coming, and Old Noshie and Skirty Marm were intensely interested in all the preparations. They had never known such a thing on Witch Island where Christmas was a day like any other. The kindly curate found some mouldy old paper chains and gave them to the witches to decorate the belfry. They were already very busy, catching bats and mixing potions for their special Christmas lunch.

Every night Old Noshie and Skirty Marm flew round the sleeping village, admiring the tinsel in the shops and peeping at everyone's Christmas trees.

One night, they found a large notice on the door of the church hall.

"'Christmas Concert at Tranters End'," read Skirty Marm. "'Come One, Come All for an Evening of Village Talent. Performers Welcome'."

"A concert!" cried Old Noshie. "What a treat! I'd love to a see a concert!"

"I've got a better idea," said Skirty Marm, who always had a better idea. "We should be in it. We could sing 'A Nasty Old Thing'. Wouldn't they all roll about laughing? Let's ask Mr Babbercorn."

But Mr Babbercorn did not like the idea at all.

"Certainly not!" he snapped. Seeing they were disappointed, he said, more gently, "Think of the fuss there would be when people saw two witches."

Old Noshie and Skirty Marm scowled.

"Nobody needs to know we live here!" argued Skirty Marm. "You could just pretend we're witches from another village."

"Other villages don't *have* witches," said Mr Babbercorn. "It's out of the question."

"Meanie!" shouted Old Noshie. "You never want us to have any fun!"

"I'm sorry, Noshie," said Mr Babbercorn, "but you must promise me not to set foot inside the church hall during the concert."

Both witches set up a howl of protest at this so he added, "I might let you watch it through the skylight in the roof – but only if you promise to be good."

Sulkily, both witches promised.

"I do hope they behave," he said to himself when he left them. "It's been so peaceful lately."

He would not have been at all happy if he had heard the conversation in the belfry after he had gone.

"That smelly spoil-sport!" grumbled Old Noshie. "Now we won't have our treat."

But Skirty Marm – that witch of great ideas – was busy thinking. Presently, she said, "There is a way we could do something at the concert."

"No, there isn't," Old Noshie said with a

sniff. "Not now we've promised to stay out of the hall."

"We don't have to go into the hall!" cackled Skirty Marm. "Listen . . . "

And she whispered her plan into Old Noshie's green ear.

Two days later, when Mr Snelling and Mr Babbercorn were sorting out the programme for the concert, Mr Snelling said, "Here's a funny thing, Cuthbert."

"What?" Mr Babbercorn was working at the typewriter.

"It's a letter from Ted Blenkinsop over at Blodge Farm." The vicar put on his glasses, to read it. "'Dere Mr Sneling I want to be in the consert. Pleese put me in as the Divine Floradora. Luv Mr Blenkinsop.' Most odd, don't you think? And the spelling is dreadful."

Mr Babbercorn was too busy to pay much attention. "Ted Blenkinsop," he said as he typed out the programme, "as the Divine Floradora."

On the night of the concert, every soul in Tranters End was packed into the hall. They wouldn't have missed this social pinnacle for the world, even if Mrs Bagg-Meanly had not ordered them all to turn up. The evil housekeeper was checking their names on a list as they came in.

Old Noshie and Skirty Marm were at the back door of the church hall, dancing with excitement. Hidden in the bushes beside them was a large, black shape.

"Do you remember what to do?" whispered Skirty Marm. "When Mrs Tucker plays your music, you dance onto the stage—"

"Of course I remember," said the mysterious shape in the bushes. "Don't fluster me."

"Come on, Skirt," nagged Old Noshie. "Let's get up on the roof before it starts."

The two witches climbed up the drainpipe and peeped through the skylight in the church hall roof, pinching each other with wicked glee.

Mr Babbercorn was standing beside the door, ready to switch off the lights.

That's strange, he thought suddenly. There's Ted Blenkinsop in the front row! Surely he's meant to be performing?

A horrible thought came into his head. He glanced up at the skylight and, to his relief, saw Old Noshie's glowing green face. No, it couldn't be anything to do with the witches. All the same, it was peculiar. Ted Blenkinsop was a stout man with a red face and a bald head. It was difficult to imagine him as the Divine Floradora. Or, indeed, as the Divine anything.

But there was no time to solve the mystery. Mr Snelling was signalling from behind the curtain. Mr Babbercorn switched off the lights. The show was beginning.

Mr Snelling loved the concert. He started it, as he did every year, by singing 'When Father Papered the Parlour', with Mrs Tucker playing the piano. The audience clapped very loudly. They were fond of their vicar and this was the only way they dared to show it.

Next, Mrs Bagg-Meanly sang 'Sweet and Low', timing the applause afterwards with her watch.

"This is it! This is it!" hissed Old Noshie.

"Ladies and gentlemen," announced Mr Snelling, "please welcome the Divine Floradora!"

Mrs Tucker struck up the music. With a loud clatter, the Divine Floradora took the stage.

"Oh my goodness!" choked Mr Snelling. There were gasps and whispers all round the church hall.

The Divine Floradora wore a silk garter on one leg and a pink rose behind one ear. She also wore scarlet lipstick and false eyelashes. Old Noshie and Skirty Marm had to pinch each other black and blue to stop laughing out loud. The Divine Floradora was a LARGE BROWN COW.

There was an even greater sensation when she stopped dancing and began – in a deep contralto voice – to sing.

"Who dances like a fairy?
Floradora!
Who is beautiful, though hairy?
Floradora!
Who dresses up in silk
And gives champagne instead of milk?
I'm referring to the lovely
Floradora!

"Who mouldered in her field
(Floradora!)
Till she practically congealed?
Floradora!
Who escaped one day for good
And went off to Hollywood?
It could only be the gorgeous
Floradora!"

The church hall seethed with excitement. The people at the back stood on their chairs to get a better view. Mr Snelling's mouth gaped open in amazement. Even Mrs Bagg-Meanly was silent.

"What on earth shall I do?" wondered Mr Babbercorn, for of course he knew who was behind this outrage.

Mrs Tucker had stopped playing the piano, but the Divine Floradora, enjoying the attention, went on kicking her front legs and stamping her hoofs.

Mrs Bagg-Meanly had recovered. She stomped onto the stage.

"Right," she said. "Let's put a stop to this."

"Go away, you rude woman!" shouted Floradora.

The church hall went deathly quiet. Everyone would have liked to laugh but did not dare.

Mrs Bagg-Meanly was furious.

"Vicar!" she roared. "Get this shameless creature off my stage!"

"Shoo!" said Mr Snelling weakly.

"Shoo yourself," replied Floradora. "How dare you speak like that to a STAR?"

But someone else was climbing onto the stage. It was Ted Bleinkinsop and he was very angry.

"Star, my foot!" he snapped. "That's no Divine Floradora – that's Nellie, my best cow!"

"I am no longer your cow," said Floradora. "I am an artiste."

This made Ted Blenkinsop even angrier.

"Take all that muck off your face, my girl, and come home to your pasture!"

"No–o–o–o–o!" cried the cow in a long moo.

"Do as you're told," said Ted Blenkinsop. "No cow of mine goes prancing about on stage like a painted hussy."

Careful not to be noticed, Mr Babbercorn slipped out of the church hall. He was just in time. Old Noshie and Skirty Marm had climbed off the roof and were trying to sneak away.

"Stop right there!" ordered Mr Babbercorn.

The witches stopped.

"I hope you're both ashamed of yourselves," said Mr Babbercorn. "You're certainly a disappointment to me."

These were terrible words. Old Noshie and Skirty Marm hung their heads sulkily.

"Do you realize what you've done?" Mr Babbercorn demanded. "Nellie is Mr Blenkinsop's favourite cow – worth a lot of money and almost one of the family. She was perfectly happy until you two came along and filled her head with silly ideas. Remove that spell at once."

The witches scowled and looked at their toes.

"It was only a joke," mumbled Skirty Marm.

"You were mean to us," said Old Noshie. "We wanted to teach you a lesson."

"The only lesson you have taught me," said Mr Babbercorn, "is that I can't trust you."

He grasped them each by their bony hands so they could not escape and marched them round to the side of the church hall. The Divine Floradora was already outside. The concert had broken up in chaos, and she was sitting in the middle of the path, refusing to budge.

"Blast it all, Nellie!" Ted Blenkinsop was shouting. "Why won't you come home?"

"Because I'm going to Hollywood to be a film star," said Floradora. "I'm bored with the farm."

"Bored!" cried Ted Blenkinsop. "Well, there's gratitude for you. I've given you everything. You've had the best field, the longest grass . . ."

Mr Babbercorn parked the witches in the laurel bushes.

"Stay there," he said, "and when I nod to you, take off the spell."

He went over to the cow and put his arm around her neck.

"Now, Nellie, listen to me," he said. "Don't you think it would be wiser to stay in Tranters End?"

"No," said the cow. "And don't call me Nellie. I'm Floradora, the Bovine Marvel."

"You've never known any other life," Mr Babbercorn said gently. "I think you'd soon want your home. And what about poor Mr

87

Blenkinsop? Think how he'd miss you. Not to mention Mrs Blenkinsop and the children."

"That's right, Nellie," said Ted Blenkinsop. "Why, if you left us it would ruin our Christmas!"

The Divine Floradora sighed. "I've been a very silly girl. How could I think of leaving my dear family? Please take me home so I can just be Nellie again!"

"That's my lass," said Ted Blenkinsop. He gave her the kind of slap on the flank that cows like.

Mr Babbercorn nodded to the witches. A few seconds later, Nellie mooed loudly. The spell had been removed and she was an ordinary cow again.

"What a relief!" Mr Blenkinsop mopped his red face. "Thanks for talking some sense into her, Mr Babbercorn. I don't know what we'd do, without our Nellie."

The Blenkinsop family led their beloved cow home.

Skirty Marm tugged at Mr Babbercorn's sleeve.

"We still think you're mean!" she announced. "You can't take a joke and you won't let us have any fun. We don't want to be your friends any more."

"So POOH TO YOU!" added Old Noshie.

The two witches stuck out their tongues and vanished into thin air.

Mr Babbercorn went very sadly back to the vicarage.

I was absolutely right to tell them off, he thought. They knew they were being naughty. But, oh dear – whatever shall I do without them?

8

Witches to the Rescue

Old Noshie and Skirty Marm were deeply offended by Mr Babbercorn's strict words. He had hurt their feelings when he said he could not trust them. For the next three days they stayed sulking in their belfry, waiting for the curate to climb the one hundred and eighty-six steps and say he was sorry.

But the days passed, and Mr Babbercorn did not come.

"What did I tell you?" sniffed Skirty Marm. "He doesn't love us any more. Let's go right back to being bad."

"It'll serve him right," said Old Noshie. "He'll have to come and see us then."

The moment it was dark, they flew out on their brooms for a game of Vests-in-the-Rain.

There was hardly any washing hanging out on the December evening so the game was not

90

much fun. They shouted "Pooh to you!" down a few chimneys, but took no relish in it. And when they returned to the belfry, sure that Mr Babbercorn would come rushing to tell them off, they were disappointed. Not even severe naughtiness had brought the curate.

"We're obviously not being bad enough," growled Skirty Marm. "We'll have to think of something worse."

"Being good was certainly very tiring," admitted Old Noshie. "But I miss our friend, Skirt. Don't you?"

"No!" said Skirty Marm. But she did not sound very sure.

"You know what, Skirt?" Old Noshie went on bravely. "I think we should go to see him. I think we're the ones who should say sorry. After all, we were pretty naughty."

"Pish and posh," said Skirty Marm proudly. "Let him apologize to us!"

"But, Skirt," Old Noshie wailed, "what if he doesn't?"

Skirty Marm thought hard. She did not want to lose their only friend, and she was secretly longing for an excuse to make it up.

"All right," she said at last. "Let's go to see

him. After all, it is nearly Christmas."

"Hurrah!" cried Old Noshie.

The witches had been very bored and lonely without Mr Babbercorn and, deep down, they knew he had been right to tell them off. Though they would never have admitted it, being bad was not as much fun as they remembered.

The minute the high street was empty, the witches flew over to the vicarage and climbed through Mr Babbercorn's bedroom window.

"Skirt, look!" whispered Old Noshie.

There, lying pale and ghastly on his lumpy bed, was the poor curate. He was so thin he looked like his own shadow.

"Oh, Mr B.!" cried Skirty Marm. "What has happened to you?"

"Witches!" Mr Babbercorn said weakly. "It's lovely to see you, but you shouldn't be here – you're in danger . . ."

"We came to say sorry," said Old Noshie in a small voice. "We'll be good for ever now. Won't we, Skirt?"

"Yes," gulped Skirty Marm.

"Old Noshie and Skirty Marm," said Mr Babbercorn, "I'm afraid I'm very ill. Mrs Bagg-Meanly has done for me at last! She made me eat

something poisonous, and I'm sinking fast—
starvation has undermined my constitution. You
have been wonderful friends. Please be kind to
the vicar, for my sake."

"We'll make you fly again," promised Old
Noshie. "We'll go back to your birthday island
and build you a little house, and you'll be right
as rain in no time."

Mr Babbercorn shook his head. "No use now.
Goodbye, my dear witches. Be good, and don't
forget me."

Big tears rolled down the faces of the two
witches. As they flew back to the belfry they

were bitterly sorry they had ever been cross with their friend.

"If only we could do something to help him!" sobbed Old Noshie. "He called us his dear witches!"

"Stop howling," said Skirty Marm, "I'm trying to think of a spell."

"There's no spell strong enough for this," said Old Noshie. "Not even in the Purple-Stocking Spellbook. It's quite useless!"

But Skirty Marm was having profound and important thoughts.

"There is one spell that would help Mr Babbercorn," she said. "MRS ABER-CROMBIE'S PRIVATE POTION!"

Old Noshie's green face turned pale. "You're a loony! The recipe's in her special spellbook – it's impossible!"

"It's our only hope," said Skirty Marm quietly. "We have to get it."

"But how, Skirt, how?" Old Noshie was shaking all over with horror.

"We'll have to fly back to Witch Island and steal it," said Skirty Marm. "We'll go tonight, when she's asleep, and look up the spell in her book. She'll never know we were there."

"What about her guards?"

"We'll biff them and tie them up," said Skirty Marm firmly.

"Biff them?" shrieked Old Noshie. "How are we going to biff huge old Purple-Stocking palace guards?"

"Suit yourself," Skirty Marm said loftily. "I'll do it on my own."

Old Noshie remembered Mr Babbercorn calling them "dear witches", and suddenly felt very brave.

"You're right – we have to take the chance. Even if we get our noses squashed," she added in a wobbly voice.

Night fell upon Tranters End. It was freezing cold and extremely dark. Their hearts thumping, the witches set out on their quest to save their friend. Never had the little village seemed so cosy and welcoming. Never had the thought of Mrs Abercrombie seemed so awful.

After several hours of fast flying they saw the looming black mountains of Witch Island. They landed silently, on the sooty beach nearest the palace, and hid their brooms under some black rocks. It felt very strange, returning to their old home which they had not expected to see for a hundred years. Although it was pitch-dark, Old Noshie and Skirty Marm knew every stone by heart.

The entrance to the palace cave was guarded by four massive Purple-Stocking witches, each holding a flaming torch.

"The back door has guards on it, too," whispered Skirty Marm. "We'll have to go down the chimney."

"We must be mad!" grumbled Old Noshie. But she followed her friend up the rough sides of the royal cave. It was a steep and painful climb. By the time they reached the chimney, they were both bruised and panting.

"Oh, stinks!" swore Old Noshie, coughing in the smoke. "The fire's still lit – we'll be burned to a crisp! Now what shall we do?"

"We'll try to land in the coal bucket," said Skirty Marm grimly. "Don't be so wet, Nosh. I'm not going to turn back now."

"Wet, am I?" snarled Old Noshie. "I'll show you!" She grabbed Skirty Marm's hand.

"One, two, three . . . jump!" cried the witches together – and they leapt boldly down the palace chimney.

As luck would have it, they landed not in the coal bucket but smack on top of an old Purple-Stocking, who was snoring beside the fire. She was squashed as flat as a pancake and knocked unconscious. It was a promising start which cheered them both enormously.

"So far, so good," said Skirty Marm. "Now, let's find Mrs Abercrombie's bedroom!"

They tiptoed through the damp, rocky corridors, following the sound of the queen's huge, rumbling snores, which shook the earth beneath their feet.

As they approached the chamber where Mrs Abercrombie lay sleeping, their teeth chattered with fear – they were not even pretending to be brave. Four more guards stood outside the queen's bed-cave, their hairy faces glaring in the light of their torches.

"It's impossible!" moaned Old Noshie.

"Shhh!" ordered Skirty Marm. "I'm thinking!"

At that moment, from a distant quarter of the great palace cave, a voice called, "Two o'clock, and all's well!"

The voice bounced off the dank stone walls, echoing and re-echoing for ages until it seemed to come from a thousand places at once.

"That's it!" exclaimed Skirty Marm. "We'll trick them!" She dragged Old Noshie into a narrow cranny in the wall.

"Ow!" complained Old Noshie. "What are you playing at?"

To her astonishment and horror, Skirty Marm threw back her head and yelled as loud as she could, "Help! Burglars! Help! Robbers! Crocodiles! Help!"

Her voice swooped and dived as if hundreds of Skirty Marms were yelling at once all over the palace.

The effect on the four guards was dramatic.

"It's over there—"

"No, over here—"

"This way, I tell you—"

They scattered in four different directions, leaving the door to the royal bed-cave unguarded.

Old Noshie and Skirty Marm wasted no time. The moment the guards were out of sight, they scuttled through the curtained archway.

"Yeuch!" Skirty Marm said feelingly.

Mrs Abercrombie lay snoring on her massive granite bed, the fat rippling all over her gigantic body. The last time the witches had seen her was at their trial. She was terrible to look upon, and the thought of poor Mr Babbercorn was all that kept them from running away.

In one corner of the gloomy cave stood a stone table. On that table lay a mighty book. They had never seen it before, but they knew only too well what it was – *Mrs Abercrombie's Private Collection of Spells*, the most magic and dangerous book in all the world.

As quietly as possible, Skirty Marm opened the vast book and began searching through the index of recipes. This was difficult because the pages were thin and crackly. However, she soon found what they had come for.

"Page 7777776," she whispered solemnly, "Mrs Abercrombie's Private Potion."

"Drat!" muttered Old Noshie, peering over her shoulder.

They had hoped just to glance at the spell and learn it by heart, but it covered a whole page of the book in tiny writing.

"Only one thing for it," said Old Noshie recklessly. "We'll have to tear the page right out and take it with us."

"Here goes!" Skirty Marm ripped out the

page and folded it safely inside her rags. "Done it!"

"YES!" rumbled a dreadful voice from the bed. "You've done it! Welcome back to Witch Island, you miserable little scoundrels!"

Mrs Abercrombie was sitting up on her cement pillows, with sparks fizzing out of her hideous mouth.

Old Noshie and Skirty Marm squealed.

"I'll boil you in oil for this!" roared Mrs Abercrombie. "How dare you steal my secret spells? Give back that page – I'm going to turn you into slugs, and I don't want tracks all over it!"

She raised her hand, and the witches gave themselves up for lost. It had all been for nothing, and they were about to become slugs.

Then, suddenly, Old Noshie shrieked, "She can't do anything – she's not wearing her hat! She's powerless without it! Run, Skirt, run!"

"Guards!" howled Mrs Abercrombie. "Where are my guards?"

Skirty Marm did a very brave thing. She ran right to the end of the queen's bed where the Power Hat hung on the bedpost, the everlasting candle burning in its point. Then she snatched the Power Hat and rammed it on her own head.

Mrs Abercrombie turned pale grey and crashed back on her bed in a dead faint. Without the Hat she was only an ordinary Purple-Stocking. Whoever wore the Power Hat was the rightful Queen of Witch Island. Her cruel reign was over.

Old Noshie and Skirty Marm dashed away down the long corridors, hooting with triumph. Time and time again the guards rushed at them, then fell back in dismay when they saw the flame of the magic hat.

"We did it!" shouted Old Noshie. "We did it!"

They ran to the beach, leapt on their brooms and zoomed away from Witch Island.

When they were well above the sea, Skirty Marm took off the Power Hat and flung it down into the waves.

Old Noshie was so staggered she almost toppled off her broom. "Why did you do that? You could have been Queen of Witch Island!"

"Pooh!" said Skirty Marm. "I don't ever want to go back there. It's a smelly place. It'll do them good to try democracy, for a change."

"Now we can stay in Tranters End for ever and ever!" said Old Noshie happily.

"Yes," said Skirty Marm. "If only . . . Oh, we haven't a minute to lose!"

9

What Happened at the Jumble Sale

There was only one hour of darkness left when the witches got back to Tranters End. Quickly, they flew among woods and hedges, picking all the herbs and berries they needed to make up Mrs Abercrombie's special potion.

Some of the ingredients were extremely strange, however, and far more difficult to find.

"'One churchwarden's toenail,'" read Old Noshie, frowning at the torn piece of paper.

"Mr Noggs is a churchwarden," said Skirty Marm.

They flew to the bedroom above the butcher's shop where Mr Noggs lay fast asleep beside his wife. Old Noshie cast a short-term sleeping spell (very simple, from the Yellow-Stocking Spell-book) and Skirty Marm pushed back Mr Noggs's duvet to snip off the nail of his left big toe.

The next ingredient on the list – "one hair of

a maiden in love" – was even easier. Belinda Tucker, the grown-up daughter of the Tuckers at the post office, was about to marry PC Bloater. The witches simply popped into the post office and plucked out one of Belinda's long brown hairs.

For "one reflection of an infant smile" they flew to Blodge Farm and caught the sweet smile of Matthew, the Blenkinsop baby, in a mirror.

The two witches were very determined and soon there was only one ingredient left on the list.

" 'A stamp'," read Old Noshie, " 'that has been licked by someone with a black heart'."

"Ha!" said Skirty Marm. "I know who has a black heart around here."

"Mrs Bagg-Meanly!" cried Old Noshie.

They flew to the bedroom window of the black-hearted housekeeper. She lay, snoring loudly, beneath a pink quilt with half a chocolate cake on the bedside table.

"You do the sleeping spell," said Skirty Marm, "and I'll get the window open. She must have a stamp around somewhere – we'll just wipe it against her tongue."

"Yuck!" grumbled Old Noshie. "I'm not doing that!"

She did not have to. On the table lay a letter, in Mrs Bagg-Meanly's writing, with a stamp already licked and stuck on the envelope. Skirty Marm snatched it, and the two friends rushed back to the belfry just as the sun was rising.

"Bother, we haven't got a cauldron," muttered Skirty Marm. "We'll have to use your hat."

By the time the sun was properly up they were hard at work, boiling and brewing and racking their brains to remember everything they had learned at witch school. This was the toughest spell they had ever tried. One by one, they dropped the ingredients into the mixture bubbling away in Old Noshie's hat.

In the early afternoon, two exhausted witches sniffed the nasty-smelling mixture.

"All ready," announced Skirty Marm. "Come on, Nosh – I don't care if anyone sees us. This is an emergency."

In fact, everyone in the village had gone to Mrs Bagg-Meanly's Christmas jumble sale, so the streets were deserted when the witches zoomed over to the vicarage, clutching the precious hatful of medicine.

Mr Babbercorn lay as they had left him,

stretched out on his bed. He was so pale and still that the witches were frightened.

"Wake up!" cried Old Noshie. "It's us! We've come to make you better!"

Mr Babbercorn only groaned.

"Deary me," said Skirty Marm, "these humans are such delicate little creatures – a puff of wind could blow them away!"

She poured a few drops of the potion down the poor curate's throat. Holding their breaths, the witches waited.

"It doesn't work!" wailed Old Noshie, starting to grizzle.

"Look!" hissed Skirty Marm.

Slowly, a change was creeping over Mr Babbercorn. First, colour surged into his thin cheeks until they were quite red and round. Then his wispy hair became thick and yellow, and his skinny arms and legs swelled with muscle. Even his shabby clothes turned glossy and new. Altogether, he was more healthy and hearty than he had ever been in his life.

Old Noshie and Skirty Marm were so astonished by the power of the potion that they shrank back against the wall as Mr Babbercorn leapt off his bed.

"Good gracious!" he exclaimed "I feel *wonderful*!"

His voice had grown stronger, too – he no longer had a weedy tenor but a rich, deep bass-baritone.

"What a beautiful day!" He flung open the window – and he was so strong that the whole thing came away in his hand.

"Hurrah!" screamed Old Noshie and Skirty Marm, breaking into a dance of delight. "It worked!"

"My dear witches," said Mr Babbercorn in his new deep voice, "how has this happened? And how can I ever thank you?"

He lifted them both into the air with one finger so that their heads bumped against the ceiling. Once their feet were back on the floor, the witches told him how they had returned to Witch Island to steal Mrs Abercrombie's spell.

Mr Babbercorn was so touched by their bravery that big, juicy tears rolled down his face.

"You'll never be able to go back to your island again," he said, "and you did it all for me!"

"Because you're our friend," said Old Noshie

107

proudly, "And we never had a proper friend before – did we, Skirt?"

"You'll be able to give that Mrs Bagg-Meanly a good biffing now," said Skirty Marm. "We never dreamed this potion would be so good. We only used a teeny drop – there's tons left."

"Is there now?" Mr Babbercorn was thoughtful. "I've got an idea. Come with me."

He picked up the two witches as if they had been as light as two feathers and carried them down the vicarage stairs, one on each shoulder. As they crossed the landing, they heard the voice of Mrs Bagg-Meanly.

She was in her bedroom, chortling to herself and singing a horrid little song:

"Har har harm, hee hee hee,
I've poisoned him and now I'm free!
Now this one's gone, I need not fear –
THEY WON'T SEND NO MORE
CURATES HERE!"

"We'll see about that!" said Mr Babbercorn.

As I have said, everyone in the village was at the jumble sale, by order of Mrs Bagg-Meanly. And a very gloomy jumble sale it was. Nobody spoke, but instead stood around the church hall in sad little groups. Mr Snelling sat behind the bric-a-brac stall, sniffing because he was so worried about his poor curate.

When Mr Babbercorn strode in, with a witch on each shoulder, there was a terrific sensation.

"Cuthbert!" gasped Mr Snelling. He jumped up so suddenly that he knocked over a "Present from Skegness" cruet on his stall. "Can this really be you?"

"It certainly is!" boomed Mr Babbercorn, gently putting down the witches.

The villagers gaped at him, unable to believe their eyes.

"But . . . but . . ." stammered Mr Snelling, "I left you lying ill in bed!"

"Well, now I'm cured," said Mr Babbercorn. "I'm as fit as a flea." To prove it, he lifted the whole bric-a-brac table in the air and held it above his head.

"Can this really be my poor young curate?" cried Mr Snelling. "Why, you're as strong as Superman!" The kind-hearted vicar blew his nose loudly, overcome with joy.

"Listen everybody," Mr Babbercorn said. "I'll explain everything later. Right now, we have work to do. We're going to overthrow the tyrant, Mrs Bagg-Meanly, and drive her out of this village for ever!"

There were murmurs of "Impossible!" and "He's gone crazy!" Tranters End without Mrs Bagg-Meanly seemed too good to be true.

While all this was going on, Old Noshie and Skirty Marm had been busy. Into the big tea urn at the back of the hall they poured the rest of Mrs Abercrombie's potion.

"You must all trust me," said Mr Babbercorn, "and do exactly as I say. First, everyone must have a cup of tea. Line up, please."

The villagers were too dazed by these strange happenings to protest. Besides, this new, dynamic curate was not the sort of person you disobeyed. They formed an orderly queue beside the urn, and Old Noshie and Skirty Marm served the tea. It had not been nice tea to begin with and the potion made it smell worse.

"Who are these two raggedy old ladies?" whispered Mrs Noggs to Mrs Tucker. "They look just like a couple of . . . well . . . witches!"

At precisely half past two, Mrs Bagg-Meanly entered the church hall. She was in high spirits, singing her little song and wondering what to wear to Mr Babbercorn's funeral. But she stopped short at the door for an extraordinary sight met her eyes.

They were all waiting for her, in a half-circle, not at all frightened. In fact, they were smiling. For the first time in her life, Mrs Bagg-Meanly felt uneasy. What could this mean?

Then two figures stepped forward. One was Mr Snelling and the other was—

"Argh!" screamed Mrs Bagg-Meanly, "You? What are you doing here? What's going on?"

She grabbed Mr Babbercorn's ear, but he

shook her off as if she had been a fly.

"What-what-what?" she choked, turning a ghastly colour. "I'm sending that poison straight back to the shop! It doesn't work and I've been tricked! Harold Snelling, I want an explanation!"

To her amazement, all Mr Snelling said was, "Shut up."

"What?" gasped Mrs Bagg-Meanly.

"I said, Shut up, Cousin Violet," said the vicar. "The worm has turned at last. You've made us all miserable for far too long. I'm in charge now – and this is my jumble sale!"

The villagers of Tranters End burst into a round of applause and there were cries of "Hear! hear!"

"So!" roared Mrs Bagg-Meanly. "You want me to lose my temper, do you?" She rolled up her sleeves, ready to fight for her power. "All right! Who wants to be first?"

"CHARGE!" shouted the vicar.

Before Mrs Bagg-Meanly knew what was happening, all the people of Tranters End were on top of her. They rolled her across the floor like a barrel, they tossed her in the air, they pinched and pummelled and tweaked and pulled, they messed up her hair and twanged her suspenders until she was shrieking for mercy.

"Stop! I'll do anything!"

"Cousin Violet," Mr Snelling said, "you have ruled Tranters End like a wicked tyrant. You have stolen my food and tried to poison my curate. But your reign of terror is over. You will pack your bags and go off to live with your sister. And if you ever set foot here again—"

"All right!" snarled Mrs Bagg-Meanly "You don't have to draw me a map, Harold. I'm going." She scrambled up, looking very sulky. "But you'll miss me – you wait and see!"

She stomped back to the vicarage to pack her bags and that was the last time her size eleven feet were ever heard in Tranters End.

There was a moment of stunned silence. Then someone shouted, "Three cheers for Mr Babbercorn!"

The cheers were so loud that the crockery on the bric-a-brac stall rattled.

Mr Babbercorn held up his hand for quiet. "Ladies and gentlemen," he said, "it isn't me you should be cheering today. Our village has been saved by two noble witches." He pulled forward Old Noshie and Skirty Marm, who blushed and looked very shy. "Old Noshie and Skirty Marm sheltered here when they were banished from their home. They risked being turned into slugs to get the magic potion that has done such wonders. Three cheers for Old Noshie and Skirty Marm!"

"Hip, hip, hurrah! Hurrah! Hurrah!" cheered everyone.

The two witches had never felt so proud and happy. They had once been wicked and played tricks on humans. Now here they were, being clapped and cheered and shaken by the hand. It was a lovely feeling.

"Why, being good is best after all!" said Old Noshie.

"I've always wanted to meet a real witch," said Mrs Tucker.

Ted Blenkinsop said, "Now I know what came over my Nellie!"

"Yes, it explains a lot," agreed Mr Snelling. "I knew a shrinking housekeeper and a singing cow couldn't be normal."

"Tell you what," cried Mr Noggs, who besides being a churchwarden was a butcher, "the vicar and Mr Babbercorn and these two magnificent witches will have the best Christmas

114

dinner this village has ever seen! My biggest turkey . . ."

"And a big box of luxury crackers," chimed in Mrs Tucker.

"And a prize-winning pudding!" cried some-one else.

Everyone began to offer delicious things to eat and drink until the hungry vicar's mouth was watering.

"You know what, Nosh?" said Skirty Marm. "I'm glad we were banished!"

"Me too," declared Old Noshie. "This is our real home now. And the humans are right – *East, West, Home's Best*!"

Mendax
the Mystery Cat

For Elsa and Claudia

1

A Strange Cat

"Drat!" swore Skirty Marm.

She threw her knitting across the belfry. The needles hit one of the huge church bells with a dull "ping".

"This is impossible!" she shouted crossly. "We want to get decent Christmas presents for our pals, and all we can do is this silly knitting! What's the point of being witches if we can't use our magic?"

"We promised Mr Babbercorn we wouldn't," Old Noshie reminded her. "We swore we'd give up magic and be terribly good when we came to live with the humans. And we don't have any money, so we'll just have to give everyone our egg cosies."

She held up her boggly piece of knitting. It looked more like a hand grenade than an egg cosy, but Old Noshie was extremely proud of it

119

– she had never made anything by herself before without using one of her spells. Secretly, she was rather sorry she had to give it away, even to Mr Babbercorn.

Mr Cuthbert Babbercorn was the young curate at the church where the witches lived, and their best friend. He had been very kind to Old Noshie and Skirty Marm since the amazing day he discovered he had two genuine witches living with (and eating) the bats in his belfry.

Skirty Marm pulled a dead bat out of her sleeve now, and swallowed it with an angry gulp.

"I did so want to get something special for Mr B. – perhaps a friendly little robot to do his shopping."

She stamped her foot impatiently, raising a little cloud of dust. She was a long, skinny witch with a wrinkled grey face, beady red eyes and a clump of purple hair. Her black rags were full of holes, and her black pointed hat was patched and sagging.

Two months before – the day after Hallowe'en – the two witches had been thrown out of their home on Witch Island for singing a rude song about their queen, the evil Mrs

Abercrombie. As part of the dreadful punishment, they had also been stripped of their stockings.

I must explain what a terrible thing this is for a witch. On Witch Island, the colour of a witch's stockings shows how old she is, and how much magic she is licensed to perform. Old Noshie and Skirty Marm were one hundred and fifty years old – very young for a witch – and at the time of their banishment they had been Red-Stockings. The Red-Stockings were wild young witches, hardly out of school. Witches over two hundred years old were Green-Stockings. And the most powerful witches of all, who were more than three hundred years old, were the Purple-Stockings. Every time a witch changed the colour of her stockings, her magic increased and she was given a more advanced spellbook.

On the miserable night when Old Noshie and Skirty Marm were banished from Witch Island, they had been in a very sad state – two failed witches without stockings, spellbooks or a home. They would have been even more miserable if they had known that their broomsticks had been instructed to drop them into the sea. The two brooms were faithful creatures, however, and though the witches never knew it, they performed one last act of kindness. Instead of letting Old Noshie and Skirty Marm drown in the freezing water, they left them in the quiet English village of Tranters End.

At first, only Mr Babbercorn had known they were living in the church belfry. Now, thanks to a series of strange, magical happenings, everyone in the village knew about their local witches. Old Noshie and Skirty Marm had been made very welcome. Their friend Mrs Tucker, who ran the post office, was also Brown Owl. She had not only given each of the witches a pair of faded red stockings to keep their legs warm, but she had also invited them to join her Brownie pack, and this was where they had learnt to knit.

"I don't know how those tiny Brownies find knitting so easy," Old Noshie complained. "I'll never get a badge at this rate."

She was shorter and fatter than Skirty Marm, with a round, bald head (on which she wore a blue wig to keep out the cold) and sticking-out ears. The most distinctive thing about Old Noshie was that her face was bright green (not an unusual colour for a witch) and glowed in the dark. She glanced up at her friend, and squeaked, "Skirty! Remember our promise to Mr B.!"

Skirty Marm was climbing up the side of one of the bells – she was extremely nimble for a witch in her 150s. From somewhere in the wooden rafters, she pulled a bottle of Nasty Medicine.

"Just a little sip," she said, "to cheer us up. It's ages since we touched a drop and we only promised not to get drunk again."

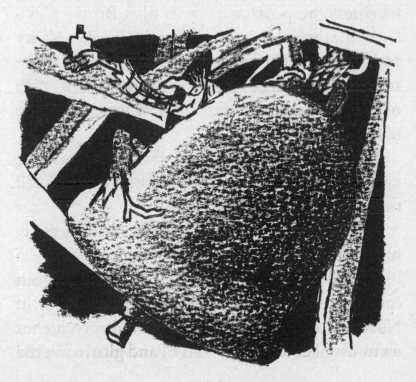

"Oh, well," said Old Noshie, "one teeny sip won't make us drunk."

Skirty Marm jumped down to the splintery wooden floor, opened the bottle, and took a swig of Nasty Medicine. As all sensible humans know, it is WICKED and DANGEROUS to drink someone else's Nasty Medicine. What is poisonous to a human, however, is often an absolute treat for a witch. Noshie and Skirty each took two large gulps.

"I feel a little better now," hiccuped Old Noshie.

"I'm still very weak and depressed," Skirty Marm said. "I'd better have some more." She took another large gulp, smacking her lips. "It's not like breaking our promise, because we actually need it."

Old Noshie said, "I think I could force back another drop – just for my health." She grabbed the bottle for a deep swig.

Skirty Marm grabbed it back. "You greedy old stink – save some for me!"

They struggled and fought and biffed each other's noses. In a very few minutes, the bottle of Nasty Medicine was empty. The two witches were disgracefully tipsy. Mr Babbercorn would have been horrified. But they were too tipsy to feel sorry for breaking their promise.

"Let's have a rest," said Skirty Marm, "and watch our tree."

Mr Babbercorn had found an old Christmas tree made of dusty tinsel. He had decorated it with some dented silver balls, and given it to the witches, who thought it was the most beautiful thing they had ever seen. They sat and gazed at it for hours on end, and had already decided not to take it down when Christmas was over.

Nasty Medicine always made Skirty Marm rather bold and adventurous. While she gazed at the tree, little red sparks were fizzing in her eyes – a sure sign that her busy brain was working.

"I'm not giving Mr Babbercorn and Mr Snelling stinky egg cosies!" she declared suddenly. (Mr Snelling was the vicar at Tranters End.) "They're going to have the very best – and that means presents made by magic!"

"They'll never let us," Old Noshie said, shaking her head. Nasty Medicine made her a little slower than usual.

Skirty Marm pinched her friend's ear to wake her up.

"Stupid, we're not going to tell them! We'll

give them our magic presents first and say sorry afterwards. They'll be too pleased to get cross."

"Well . . ." It was never difficult to lead Old Noshie astray. She and Skirty Marm had been best friends since they were baby Yellow-Stockings, still at Elementary Witch School. They did everything together. "What do you think we should give them?"

"Nothing too elaborate," Skirty Marm said. "We haven't got our Red-Stocking Spellbooks, after all. We don't want to do anything that's going to go wrong."

She frowned. Giving up magic had not been easy for Skirty Marm. She often wished she had thought of sneaking a spellbook out of Witch Island. At school, she had won the Spellbinders Medal for thirty-six years in a row. Living as an ordinary human sometimes seemed like a bit of a comedown.

Old Noshie, who had never won any medals, did not mind so much. She added a couple of huge stitches to her egg cosy.

"Mr B. won't be cross as long as our magic presents are useful," she said comfortably.

Skirty Marm had begun to pace up and down.

"What about shoes with wings? No – they'd only make Mr B. nervous."

The two witches poured themselves cups of warm rainwater. Old Noshie produced some salted beetles she had roasted in the vicar's oven, and they settled down to think.

"I know what Mr Snelling would like!" shouted Skirty Marm suddenly. "He's always saying his bald patch makes his head cold. Let's give him some hair!"

Old Noshie was impressed. "Brilliant. He'll be so pleased. But Mr B. doesn't need hair. What'll we make for him?"

"Mr Babbercorn needs an umbrella that never gets lost," Skirty Marm said. "He told me so, only this morning. He keeps leaving them behind."

Old Noshie's bright green face was anxious. "Are they difficult spells, Skirt?"

Skirty Marm liked to think she remembered most of her Red-Stocking spells – especially when she had been at the Nasty Medicine.

"Oh, they're easy-peasy," she said grandly. "Even you could manage them. The hair spell's just a rhyme and a couple of dead newts, and the umbrella will only need basic Supernatural Animation. I got one of my medals for that, don't forget – when I made that automatic toad-skinner that washed itself up afterwards."

Above their heads, the big church clock chimed six. The noise made the whole tower shake. A human would have found the racket unbearable (poor Mr Babbercorn had been in bed for a week after accidentally hearing it at close range) but the witches liked a good loud racket.

"Great," said Skirty Marm. "It's time for Cook With Enid."

Cook With Enid was the witches' favourite television programme. They had become very keen on television while living among humans.

Old Noshie looked worried again. "Should we tell Mr B. about the Nasty Medicine?"

"No," Skirty Marm said firmly. "It would only worry the poor thing."

Feeling very considerate, they ran down the one hundred and eighty-six belfry steps to the red-brick vicarage next door. Here Mr Babbercorn lived, with Mr Snelling. When Noshie and Skirty first arrived at Tranters End, the vicar and curate had led a miserable life. An evil housekeeper, named Mrs Bagg-Meanly, had nearly starved poor, weedy Mr Babbercorn to death. Very bravely, the witches had returned to Witch Island, to steal the recipe for the magic potion that had saved his life. It had made him strong enough to drive out Mrs Bagg-Meanly and force her to get a job far away on a penguin-station in the Antarctic, but the super-strength had only been temporary. Though Mr Babbercorn's health was much better, he was still a thin, pale and generally weedy young man.

The witches found him in the kitchen, washing up the tea things.

He gave them a misty smile, through his steamed-up glasses. "Hello, witches."

Mr Snelling called from the sitting room, "Hurry up! It's starting!"

The plump vicar loved Cook With Enid. Every week, a smiling lady named Enid produced delicious food, which made his greedy mouth water. This week, she was showing viewers how to make a gigantic Christmas cake. Mr Snelling sat on his sofa with a witch on either side, happily watching Enid's clever tricks with marzipan.

Unfortunately, just at the fascinating moment when Enid was about to spread the white icing, Mr Babbercorn put his head round the sitting-room door.

"Vicar, there's a funny noise outside."

Mr Snelling sighed. "What sort of noise?"

"That's the strangest thing," said Mr Babbercorn. "I could have sworn I heard someone shouting 'Help', but when I opened the back door, nobody was there. And now it's become the most ghastly wailing and howling . . ."

"It might be burglars," Skirty Marm said hopefully. "Shall I scare them off with a bit of magic?"

"NO!" said the vicar and the curate together.

Followed closely by the nosy witches, they went into the kitchen.

"Listen," said Mr Babbercorn, beginning to tremble.

Outside the back door, they all heard a wild, wavering cry. It curdled their blood, like the sound of fingernails on a blackboard. What terrible beast could be lurking in the dark December night?

Mr Snelling, who was rather a coward, picked up the rolling pin to defend himself. "It's a ghost . . . a murderer . . ."

Mr Babbercorn, who was doing his best to be brave, said, "Don't be silly, Vicar, there hasn't been a murder in this village for four hundred years!"

"Then we must be about due for another one!" squeaked Mr Snelling.

Mr Babbercorn nervously opened the back door. A gust of freezing air blew into the kitchen.

"AARGH!" screamed the two witches. They flew up into the air and cowered against the celling in terror.

"Good gracious!" said Mr Babbercorn.

On the doorstep, looking very small and skinny and shivery, was a little black cat. It gazed around, with big green eyes, and sneezed.

Mr Snelling had a very kind heart, even when interrupted in the middle of Cook With Enid. He dropped the rolling pin, bent down, and scooped the black cat into his arms.

"Why, you poor little fellow! Poor, cold, hungry little chap! Oh, Cuthbert – isn't he sweet?"

Mr Babbercorn seized each witch by a ragged shoe, and pulled them down to the floor.

"What on earth is the matter?"

Old Noshie's bright green face had paled to the colour of pea soup.

"We . . . we don't like cats," she whispered.

Mr Babbercorn sniffed suspiciously, and looked stern.

"Have you two been breaking any promises?"

"Who – us?" shouted Skirty Marm, very offended.

"Please don't lie, Skirty. You absolutely reek of Nasty Medicine."

Skirty Marm stamped her foot. "I'm not telling you anything until you take that nasty creature away!"

"What, this cat?" Mr Babbercorn was puzzled. "I thought witches loved cats!"

"Sneaky, shifty things," muttered Skirty Marm.

"Didn't you have cats on Witch Island?"

"Only the cat-slaves," Old Noshie said.

"The what?"

"The cat-slaves are very clever. Only the Purple-Stockings are allowed to keep them." Old Noshie shuddered. "Us young witches are scared of them. The Purples send them to spy on us. Skirt pulled a cat-slave's tail once – she had to go to prison for a week."

"I did not pull his tail!" Skirty Marm roared. "I was framed!"

"But what do they do, exactly?" asked the vicar.

"It depends what you can afford," Skirty Marm said. "The expensive cat-slaves do advanced magic and gourmet cooking. The cheap models scrub out the cauldrons and sweep the chimneys."

The little black cat mewed and nestled his head into Mr Snelling's plump neck. The vicar and the curate smiled.

"This cat won't hurt you," said Mr Babbercorn kindly. "He's obviously just an ordinary little animal, with no magic about him

133

at all. In the world of humans, cats are simply harmless, furry pets. They're our friends."

Mr Snelling chuckled. "This one already wants to be my friend and I haven't even given him a saucer of milk!"

"Don't give it anything," warned Skirty Marm, "or you'll never get rid of it." She glared at the cat to show she wasn't scared.

"I don't want to get rid of him," Mr Snelling said tenderly. "I'm going to call him Tibbles."

In the days leading up to Christmas, while Tibbles settled cosily into the vicarage, the witches worked hard at their magic presents. Mr Babbercorn had said nothing more about the Nasty Medicine, and they both felt guilty about breaking their promise. This made them especially eager to make his Christmas gift perfect. Night after night, when the countryside was cloaked in darkness, they fluttered around the hedges and ditches on their broomsticks (the new ones they had trained in Tranters End) gathering dead newts, spiders' webs, bat spit and owls' feathers.

To their great annoyance, the cosiness of Tibbles the cat was increasing every day. Mr

134

Snelling fed him on chicken and cream and let him sit on his lap while he wrote his sermons. Tibbles slept in Mr Snelling's bedroom, on a tartan cat duvet. He ate out of a blue china bowl, and wore a smart red suede collar.

"It's ridiculous," said Skirty Marm scornfully. "He's totally silly about that little squirt!"

Mr Babbercorn was not quite so silly about Tibbles, but even he bought him a toy mouse and a squeaky rubber model of the Prime Minister's head. As far as the witches were concerned, Tibbles was being treated like a prince.

"I don't trust that cat," Skirty Marm said. "His eyes are too close together."

"It's not fair!" sniffed old Noshie. "Mr B. never gave us a squeaky Prime Minister!"

Mr Babbercorn saw that the witches were jealous of Tibbles.

"I know we make a fuss of him," he said, "but that's how decent human beings treat dumb animals. He's weak and timid, and we enjoy protecting him. But he can never be a real friend – not like you witches."

This slightly comforted Old Noshie and Skirty Marm, but it did not make them any fonder of Tibbles. He strolled about as if he owned the place. Once or twice, they even caught him in their private belfry.

"Of all the cheek!" grumbled Old Noshie. "You'd better count the mice, Skirt, to see if he's nicked any."

"Humans might like these smelly little animals," Skirty Marm said darkly, "but I'm not a human. I can't forget that on Witch Island a cat only means one thing!"

"A week in prison?" suggested Old Noshie.

"Trouble," said Skirty Marm.

2

An Even Stranger Christmas

Old Noshie sat on the belfry windowsill, watching the Eastern horizon. The moment the red rim of the sun appeared, she shouted: "Merry Christmas, Skirt! Let's open our presents!"

"Merry Christmas, Nosh," said Skirty Marm. "Deary me, it's almost a pity to take off that lovely paper. Don't tear it – we might want to frame it later."

The day before, Mr Babbercorn had placed three presents under the witches' tree – one square parcel from him, and two large squashy ones from Mr Snelling. They were wrapped in red paper with pictures of holly and robins on it. The witches had been up all night, gazing at the parcels. Both were far too excited to sleep. There was no such thing as Christmas on Witch Island, and they were fascinated by every detail.

Dancing and chuckling and pinching each other, they opened their first ever Christmas presents. Mr Snelling had given them each a cushion. Old Noshie's was green to match her face, and Skirty Marm's was purple to tone with her hair. They spent a happy half hour sitting on them, cuddling them and deciding where they looked handsomest.

"Even Mrs Abercrombie doesn't own a real, comfy cushion," Skirty Marm said, with deep satisfaction.

Old Noshie shivered. The very sound of the queen's name seemed to cast a shadow across the belfry. Mrs Abercrombie was the fattest, ugliest, wickedest old witch in the world. She would never forgive Old Noshie and Skirty Marm for singing the rude song about her – and she would certainly be dreaming of revenge for the TERRIBLE THING the friends had done to her when they returned to Witch Island to steal the potion recipe. Thanks to this TERRIBLE THING, Mrs Abercrombie's magic was no longer unbeatable and stupendous. But she was nearly a thousand years old, and horribly clever. The two exiled witches were still afraid of her.

"Never mind Mrs A.," said Old Noshie,

"Let's open our other present."

They opened Mr Babbercorn's parcel, and were so delighted that they were speechless for ten whole minutes. The curate had given his friends a fabulous transistor radio. It was neat and shiny, and far smarter than the clumsy radio sets on Witch Island.

Skirty Marm reverently switched it on. The witches sat on their cushions and listened to the news.

"Wonderful," sighed Skirty Marm. "D'you know, Nosh, I've never been happier in my life?"

"Now let's do our presents from each other," said Old Noshie. "Then we can go round to the vicarage. Oh, do hurry! I can't wait to give the vicar and Mr B. their magic things!"

They had been very careful to test the magic presents, to make sure nothing could possibly go wrong. Mr Snelling's hair-potion had been tried out on the bald head of Old Noshie, and they were sure he would love the rich chestnut curls they had chosen for him. Mr Babbercorn's talking umbrella, trained to call "Don't forget me!" if left behind, was a model of discretion and obedience.

"I think," said Skirty Marm, "we may feel quietly proud."

Their presents to each other were not surprises. They had decided to give each other their egg cosies to use as nose-warmers. Old Noshie and Skirty Marm put them on, admired their reflections in a scrap of tinfoil, and went down the one hundred and eighty-six belfry steps feeling very festive and elegant.

This was a special Christmas at the vicarage – not only the witches' first, but the first the vicar and Mr Babbercorn had spent without their

wicked housekeeper, Mrs Bagg-Meanly. Last Christmas, Mrs Bagg-Meanly (who was, unfortunately, the vicar's cousin) had cooked them a fish finger and two mouldy sprouts each. This year, the vicarage was crammed with delicious food. The witches found Mr Snelling chuckling over a newspaper called Antarctic News.

"Ha ha, Cousin Violet's in prison for eating penguins! Merry Christmas, witches!"

"Merry Christmas, witches," said Mr Babbercorn who was busy putting the turkey in the oven. He added politely, "What lovely nose-warmers." He had already warned Mr Snelling not to laugh.

"Thanks for our presents," beamed Old Noshie. "We just love them – don't we, Skirt?"

"They're PERFECT," said Skirty Marm. "Now, will you please open ours before church?"

"Oh, you shouldn't have," said the vicar, opening his rather untidy parcel which was wrapped in an old paper bag.

"My favourite chocolate!" He began to eat it at once.

The witches giggled and nudged each other hard. Little did Mr Snelling know that his

141

chocolate had been laced with hair potion.

"A new umbrella! How excellent," said Mr Babbercorn. His present was wrapped in a copy of the parish magazine. "Just what I needed! You know I'm always losing them."

"You won't lose this one!" giggled Old Noshie.

"Shhhh!" hissed Skirty Marm.

They were laughing so hard, they could hardly stand up.

Two very hilarious witches followed the vicar and curate into St Tranter's Church for the Christmas morning service.

The trouble began when the village children had finished their nativity play, and the vicar climbed into the pulpit, to give his sermon.

"Dear friends," he began, "On this special morning, do you ever pause to think . . ."

Mr Babbercorn hid a yawn behind his hand. He was fond of the vicar, but nobody could call his sermons interesting. They always had to have a very loud hymn afterwards to wake everyone up. He began to worry about the lunch, and hoped the turkey was all right.

He was startled out of his worrying by a yelp

from the vicar. The people in the congregation were staring up at him, their mouths open in amazement.

Mr Snelling was clutching his bald head with both hands.

"Good gracious . . ." he gasped. "Good heavens . . ."

Before the astonished eyes of the village, a soft fuzz was appearing on the vicar's bald patch. As everyone watched, it thickened into glossy chestnut curls. Then it grew into long ringlets which hung down to Mr Snelling's shoulders.

Of course, Mr Babbercorn knew who was responsible. So did the villagers. Some were shocked, some were laughing, all were looking round at the two witches who were hiding their faces in their hats.

The hair would not stop growing. It snaked and spiralled past the vicar's waist. It grew past his knees, and slowly began to pile up around his feet. As the poor vicar quavered, "Help! Help!" it crept down the pulpit steps like treacle.

That terrible pair, thought Mr Babbercorn. How could they break their promise in this naughty way?

He stood up, and glared very sternly across

the church at Old Noshie and Skirty Marm.

"Ladies and gentlemen," he said, "please keep calm. It seems that our two local witches have got rather carried away with the Christmas spirit. Noshie and Skirty, remove that spell at once!"

Skirty Marm leapt to her feet. "You don't understand!" she wailed. "It wasn't meant to do that!"

She was interrupted by a sudden loud banging on the church door, which made the whole building tremble. Several people screamed.

From the other side of the door, a shrill voice – unlike any human voice – yelled, "Let me in! He's forgotten me! He'll get rained on and I'll blame myself!"

Old Noshie knocked Skirty Marm's hat off, shouting, "You smelly old fool! That's the last time I trust one of your rubbishy spells!"

Skirty Marm knocked Old Noshie's hat off and stamped on it. "I won the Spellbinder's Medal thirty-six times. This is your fault!"

There were louder screams, as a window at the back of the church suddenly shattered. In a shower of broken glass, something leapt into the aisle. To the gasping astonishment of everyone, including the witches, a tall green umbrella was running along the aisle on spindly metal legs. Mr Noggs, the churchwarden, began to chase the umbrella. The children clapped and laughed and yelled, "Come on, brolly! Don't let him get you!"

Once he had recovered from the first, awful shock, Mr Babbercorn rushed to help Mr Noggs. He grabbed his new umbrella firmly round the middle, just as it shouted, "You idiot! You forgot me!" and tried to put itself up.

It wriggled and struggled. One of its spokes broke free, and jabbed Mr Noggs's hand.

"Ow!" he cried. "It bit me! Let's get it into the vestry!"

Mr Babbercorn and Mr Noggs, cheered on by the whole congregation, managed to carry the fighting umbrella through the vestry door.

"Let me go!" it shrieked. "Unhand me!"

They shut it into the cupboard where the spare hymn books were kept, and locked the door securely. When they returned to the church, everyone applauded.

Mr Babbercorn wiped his brow. This was a disaster. The Christmas service was in chaos. The screams of the enchanted umbrella could be heard from the vestry. Mr Snelling, wrapped in miles and miles of hair, looked like a huge fly trapped in an enormous spider's web. His hair had grown all the way down the pulpit steps and into the front pew. Ted Blenkinsop, from Blodge Farm, was trying to beat it back with a kneeling-cushion.

The two witches were roaring at each other furiously, in a storm of biffs.

"Stupid old know-it-all! You forgot those spells!" shouted Old Noshie.

"Don't you go blaming me!" shouted Skirty Marm. "You don't even remember how to scrub out a cauldron!"

Mr Babbercorn stepped over the vicar's hair, marched down the aisle, and grabbed each witch by a bony wrist. He looked so solemn that the shouts and laughter died away at once.

"Witches, I'm ashamed of you. Remove those spells this instant!"

"Tell me the truth," Mr Babbercorn said, when they were all back in the vicarage. "Have you two been drinking Nasty Medicine again? I know I smelt it on you the other day."

"That was our last bottle," cried Skirty

Marm. Both witches were weeping. "We haven't touched a drop since! Honest!"

"Well, that's something, I suppose," sighed Mr Babbercorn. "But witches, how could you disrupt our Christmas service? I thought we'd agreed – no more magic."

"Don't be too hard on them," begged soft-hearted Mr Snelling. Now that his dreadful hair had gone, he felt sorry for the two disgraced witches. After they had removed their spells, Mr Babbercorn had sent them out of the church. Their ear-splitting howls and sobs outside the door had drowned out "O Little Town of Bethlehem" and made everyone very depressed.

"We didn't mean to!" yelled Old Noshie.

"It was meant to be a lovely surprise!" sobbed Skirty Marm. "We only wanted to get you special presents. We never dreamed those dratted spells could go so wrong!"

"It was a kind thought," said Mr Snelling, giving each witch a tissue. "After all, you do keep losing your umbrellas, Cuthbert – and I certainly need more hair." He chuckled suddenly. "Just not quite so much of it."

Mr Babbercorn had meant to be very stern, but when he remembered the look on the vicar's face as the chestnut ringlets cascaded over his shoulders, he could not help laughing. He and the vicar burst into such a fit of giggles that Tibbles jumped off Mr Snelling's lap and hid under the sofa.

"We're so sorry!" moaned Skirty Marm. "We didn't mean to ruin Christmas!"

"You haven't ruined it," Mr Babbercorn said, wiping his eyes. He was extremely fond of the two witches and didn't want to hurt their feelings. "I don't believe you meant any harm. Let's pretend it didn't happen, and have a good time. It's still Christmas Day."

Old Noshie sniffed. "We'll never touch magic again. Will we, Skirt?"

"Never!" said Skirty Marm.

"Have you ever heard of piecrust promises?" Mr Babbercorn asked.

The witches shook their heads.

"A piecrust promise is easily made, and easily broken." His voice was kind, but very serious. "No more promises like piecrusts, eh? This one should be a lot stronger."

Both witches looked even more ragged than usual. Their pointed hats were boggled out of shape from fighting and crying, and bent over like two Leaning Towers of Pisa.

"We promise!" they chorused.

Then Mr Snelling cheered them all up by producing the box of deluxe crackers Mrs Tucker had given him. Old Noshie and Skirty Marm had never seen a Christmas cracker before, and were quickly distracted from their grief – Skirty particularly liked the bangs because they seemed to annoy Tibbles. Inside the crackers were gifts, jokes and paper hats. Old Noshie got a tiny sewing-kit, and Skirty Marm was delighted with her little penknife.

After this, the rest of Christmas Day was filled with happiness. The witches and their friends ate a huge lunch. They played blow-football and watched the Queen's Speech on television. Both witches were intrigued to find the human queen so much better-looking than Mrs Abercrombie.

"She talks better, too," said Old Noshie. "She didn't even scream once!"

That evening, the witches returned to their belfry contented, exhausted, and full of mince pies.

"Very tasty," said Old Noshie. "Those humans have some good ideas about food."

Skirty Marm was sitting thoughtfully on her new cushion.

"Nosh," she said, "I still don't understand how those spells went so wrong. We were so careful to test them and to make sure we had the recipe right."

Old Noshie yawned loudly, and arranged her sewing-kit and paper crown where she could see them from her bed on the floor.

"Maybe we used the wrong sort of newts," she said.

Skirty Marm shook her head stubbornly. "Those spells were easy stuff, and I know I got them right. Any little Yellow-Stocking could have done them without looking in the book." She frowned. "Do you think our magic could be wearing out?"

3

Havoc

Boxing Day began quietly in Tranters End. Mr Babbercorn took the early service, and the only other people in church were a deaf old lady named Miss Venables, and Mr Noggs.

Mr Noggs had a plaster on his hand where the enchanted umbrella had stabbed him the day before. He was a cross, stuffy sort of man, and he looked very stern.

After the service, when the curate had shouted "GOOD MORNING" to Miss Venables, Mr Noggs said, "I'd like a word with you, Mr Babbercorn."

"Of course, Mr Noggs."

"Nobody likes a joke more than I do," said Mr Noggs, "but jokes do not belong at divine service. It's not seemly, Mr Babbercorn. I hope we're not going to see any more funny business from those witches of yours."

"The witches have given me their solemn word," Mr Babbercorn assured him. "They swear they've given up magic for ever, and I believe them. This time they've turned over a new leaf. We won't see any more strange sights."

Unfortunately, it was at this exact moment that Mr Babbercorn saw a very strange sight indeed. A pair of long underpants (pale blue, with a double cuff) was dancing up the deserted village street.

It was the sort of sight that would make most people faint with shock and amazement. Most people, however, do not have Mr Babbercorn's

experience of magic. All he felt was a terrible dismay.

"I don't believe it!" he said to himself. "The witches have broken their promise!" And he had been so sure their repentance had been real. He tried to think of some other reason for a pair of dancing pants – but what other reason could there be?

With a heavy heart, he watched as Mr Noggs turned round and saw the pants skipping along the top of the churchyard wall.

"What's going on?" he spluttered furiously. "Those are mine! Those are my warm thermals for market day!" Besides being a churchwarden, Mr Noggs was the village butcher. "You come back here!" he shouted at his thermals.

The pants danced insolently towards him – then jumped away again and whisked round the bend in the lane.

Mr Noggs turned angrily to Mr Babbercorn. "This is just the sort of thing I mean," he said. "Your witch-pals have used their spells to damage my property!"

"Let's not be hasty!" begged Mr Babbercorn. "I'm sure there's a perfectly reasonable explanation—"

"Like what?" shouted Mr Noggs. "Have any more witches moved into the village since yesterday?"

"Help!" shrieked a voice. It belonged to Mrs Noggs, wife of the churchwarden and butcher.

"Vera!" gasped Mr Noggs. "Whatever are you doing?"

Mrs Noggs was clasped in the arms of a large striped shirt. It was bouncing her along the street so violently that her grey curls jiggled.

"Help!" she shrieked again as the shirt bounced her saucily past the church.

Mr Noggs and Mr Babbercorn raced after it. The striped shirt seemed to know it was being chased. First, it bounced faster. Then, it suddenly dropped Mrs Noggs in a breathless heap, and darted away. It stood on a fence, flapping gently in the breeze, and Mr Babbercorn could have sworn it was laughing at them. He could not understand why Old Noshie and Skirty Marm had returned to their old, witchy ways. This was as bad as their very first days in the village.

"I'm afraid it looks simply awful," he said to himself sadly. "Not only piecrust promises, but crocodile tears as well. Oh, witches, how could you do this to me?"

Mrs Noggs, dusting herself down, was telling her husband what had happened.

"They all jumped out of the dryer – vests, pants, two new pillowcases, all my best tea towels – they ran round the kitchen, pulling everything off the shelves, making a horrible mess. Then one of the tea towels got the back door open! Out ran all my washing – and that striped shirt of yours made a grab for me."

She and Mr Noggs glared accusingly at Mr Babbercorn.

"I suppose those witches think it's funny," said Mrs Noggs crossly, "when decent people have to chase their own underwear."

What could Mr Babbercorn say? This was, indeed, exactly the sort of thing his witches found funny. If it hadn't been happening to a very angry churchwarden, the curate would have found it rather funny himself. As it was, he felt like crying with worry.

"I'll come home with you," he said, "and take a look at the damage. Perhaps it was a spell that went wrong – or an old, leftover spell that went bad."

Mr and Mrs Noggs lived above their butcher's

shop in the little high street of Tranters End. Mr Babbercorn turned pale when he saw the angry crowd gathered outside the shop. The moment they saw the witches' best friend, everyone started shouting at once.

The Noggs's washing had been running amok. Mrs Tucker had a pillowcase hiding up her chimney. Her next door neighbour had been locked in her own shed by two tea towels, and poor Miss Venables had been knocked down by a gang of socks.

"It's a DISGRACE!" thundered Mrs Noggs.

Mr Babbercorn hung his head. Things were looking very bad indeed.

"We welcomed those witches to this village," Mrs Tucker said indignantly, "and this is how they repay us! To think of all the trouble I took teaching those two old barnacles how to knit! Well, I'm not having characters like that in my Brownie pack!"

"First they cause mayhem at the Christmas service," Mr Noggs chimed in, "and now we're all being terrorized by my washing. It won't do, Mr Babbercorn!"

Several voices shouted, "Hear! Hear!"

"We don't mind having witches here, as long

as they can live with us peacefully," Mr Noggs went on. "But we won't put up with mischief like this!"

"I can only say," Mr Babbercorn murmured apologetically, "that I am amazed and horrified, and I'll make sure everything is put right at once—"

"You'd better!" said Mr Noggs. "Because if you're too soft on those witches of yours, I'LL HAVE THE LAW ON THEM!"

Mr Babbercorn plodded back to the vicarage with a heart as heavy as a tombstone. He dreaded facing the witches, and he dreaded telling kind Mr Snelling that they seemed to have returned to a witchy life of crime.

The vicar was in the kitchen, slicing cold turkey for Tibbles. The little black cat sat on his shoulder, his eyes unblinking circles of bright green, as Mr Babbercorn poured out what had happened.

"Impossible!" cried Mr Snelling. "I refuse to believe it! There must be some mistake!"

"I'm afraid we have to face it," Mr Babbercorn said. He blew his nose. "They've let us down."

Mr Snelling collapsed heavily into a chair.

"We must all remember," he said in a shaky voice, "that Skirty and Noshie are only very young witches. We must make allowances. We must be forgiving."

"Of course I forgive them," Mr Babbercorn said. "But everyone in the village is furious. If we just forgive the witches straight away, they'll be more furious than ever. What on earth are we going to do?"

There was a knock at the back door. Mr Babbercorn opened it to find PC Bloater, the village policeman, on the step. His normally smiling face was cold and stern.

"Sorry to bother you, Mr Babbercorn" – he did not look very sorry – "but I'd like you to come down to Blodge Farm. There's been an – an incident which you might be able to explain."

"What sort of incident?" asked Mr Snelling.

Mr Babbercorn did not need to ask. He could guess.

"All right, Officer," he said with a feeble smile, "I'll come quietly."

Tibbles let out a sharp mew, leapt off the vicar's shoulder, and streaked away in the direction of the garden shed.

"I'll come too," said the vicar, grabbing his scarf.

PC Bloater usually travelled on a bicycle. Today he had a police car, sent from the nearest town. The vicar and the curate got in, trying not to feel like criminals. On the way to Blodge Farm, they could not help hearing the messages that were coming in over the car radio.

It added up to a terrible list of mischievous magic. Most of the Noggs's washing had been rounded up, but some of the socks had escaped and were still at large. Three vests had barricaded themselves into someone's barn. Someone else's herd of cows had shrunk to the size of mice, run into the kitchen, and hidden under the fridge. The district nurse had been turned into a goat. This was magic run mad. Mr Babbercorn and Mr Snelling began to wish they had never allowed witches into their belfry.

At Blodge Farm, they found a scene of confusion. A fire engine stood beside a huge old oak tree. The firemen had run a long ladder up into the tree. Three of them were standing on the ladder, holding a large net.

Ted Blenkinsop, who owned the farm, was out in the lane, dancing with fury. He was a round

159

man with a red face – and when he saw Mr Babbercorn, his red face became absolutely puce.

"Tell them to take off that spell!" he shouted. "This is a disgrace!"

"Calm down, Ted," said his wife, bouncing baby Matthew on her hip. "You'll do yourself an injury."

The three older Blenkinsop children were sitting in a row on the fence, screaming with happy laughter.

"What seems to be the trouble?" asked Mr Snelling.

"THAT!" roared Ted Blenkinsop. He pointed up into the branches of the oak tree. Through the leaves, they could just see a fireman struggling with something.

"Look out!" he called. "I've lost him!"

Something very big and weighty – it appeared to be some kind of gigantic bird – was fluttering and crashing in the branches. With a tremendous snapping of wood, it broke free and soared into the sky.

"Oh, crikey," muttered the vicar, "they've done it now!"

It was a fat, muddy pig with (Mr Babbercorn turned quite faint with astonishment) a huge

pair of wings. It swooped and curvetted through the chilly air, snorting gleefully. Another winged pig burst out of the tree. The firemen hurried down the ladder.

"Look out!" yelled Ted Blenkinsop, throwing himself down on the ground.

"ARGH!" yelled the vicar and the curate as two pigs zoomed towards them. They dropped down into the mud, and just missed being knocked senseless by a ton of flying bacon.

The winged pigs hovered over the fence. They had zoomed down because the Blenkinsop children were holding out handfuls of acorns.

"Stop that, you cheeky things," said their mother.

While the pigs were chomping acorns, the firemen tried creeping up behind them with the net. The pigs squealed, and fluttered up into the air like a pair of vast, obese pigeons.

The vicar, the curate and Ted Blenkinsop were peeling themselves out of the mud. Mr Babbercorn's glasses had fallen in a cow-pat, and he had to clean them with his muddy handkerchief before he could see a thing.

"Get my pigs back!" gasped Ted Blenkinsop. "Those animals are worth a fortune!"

"They're on the dairy roof," said Mrs Blenkinsop. "And— Oh! Look what's happened now!"

Everyone gaped. Without warning, the pigs had lost their wings. They were ordinary pigs again, very alarmed to find themselves marooned on the roof of the dairy.

The firemen moved their fire engine and put the ladder up against the wall. More messages came through on the radio in the police car. The tiny cows had also returned to normal – unfortunately, in their owner's kitchen. The goat had changed back into the district nurse. The Noggs's crazed clothes had changed back into ordinary laundry. People kept finding socks and vests in very odd places for weeks afterwards.

The attack of magic was over.

"I know who did this!" Ted Blenkinsop said furiously. He turned to Mr Babbercorn. "They've upset my valuable pigs and bust the slates on my dairy. I'LL HAVE THE LAW ON YOUR WITCHES!"

Mr Babbercorn wished people would stop calling them his witches as if he owned them. Frankly, at this moment, he would have loved to swear he did not even know them.

"Those pigs certainly did a lot of damage while they were flying about," said PC Bloater. "Criminal damage, I should say."

"Oh, Officer!" protested the vicar, "You can't arrest two pigs!"

PC Bloater said, "I didn't mean the pigs."

"You can't mean . . ." Mr Babbercorn had turned as white as his collar. "You're not going to arrest the witches?"

Through all this drama, Old Noshie and Skirty Marm had been pottering quietly round the belfry. Both were tired after the excitement of their first Christmas Day. Skirty Marm sat on her new cushion, listening to Classic FM on the new radio and feeling very cultured. Old Noshie put together a light lunch of cold mice and privet-hedge salad.

"Something simple," she said, "after all that rich human grub."

After lunch, they neatly licked their plates.

"Oh, good," said Skirty Marm, "I can hear the vicar and Mr B. coming up. Put the kettle on, Nosh." The witches did not like tea, but they did enjoy warm rainwater from the gutter.

In came Mr Babbercorn and Mr Snelling, hanging their heads. They could not look the witches in the eye, and their faces were full of sorrow.

"Hello," beamed Old Noshie. "Would you like a nice cup of rainwater?"

"Oh, witches," Mr Babbercorn burst out, "I'm not angry with you – I forgive you – but I am so dreadfully disappointed!"

"Dreadfully!" echoed Mr Snelling in a wretched voice. "Why did you do it when everything was going so well for you?"

Old Noshie and Skirty Marm had no idea what he was talking about, but they knew something was very wrong. Skirty Marm pulled her battered pointed hat straight, and folded her arms.

"Do what?" she asked.

Mr Babbercorn groaned. "Don't add to your crimes, by pretending you don't know!"

PC Bloater – red and puffing from the one hundred and eighty-six steps – stepped into the belfry.

"Old Noshie and Skirty Marm," he said solemnly, "you are under arrest."

The witches opened their mouths but no

sound came out. They were flabbergasted. Old Noshie's blue wig shifted as her bald head furrowed all over with wrinkles. Dangerous red sparks began to fizz in Skirty Marm's eyes.

"We only drunk the Nasty Medicine because we were depressed!" she shouted. "We needed it!"

"We're not talking about the Nasty Medicine," whispered Mr Babbercorn.

PC Bloater read from his notebook. "'You are charged with criminal damage caused by malicious casting of spells – such as giving wings to pigs, shrinking cows, and bringing items of clothing to life. You're also charged with assault upon the person of the district nurse.'"

"I say!" protested Mr Snelling. "Assault's a bit strong, isn't it?"

"While she was a goat, she ate a magazine," said PC Bloater. "She's feeling awful."

"Well, we're innocent," Skirty Marm said proudly. "We didn't cast any of those spells. We've spent the whole morning up here!"

"That's right," said Old Noshie. "We've got a halibut."

"I think," said Mr Babbercorn wearily, "you mean alibi. But being up here has never stopped you casting spells before. Oh, witches, how could you?"

Old Noshie's mouth began to wobble. "Why do you just assume it was us who did that magic? It's not fair!"

"You old fool," said Skirty Marm. "Who else around here does magic? No wonder they blame us. And now the vicar and Mr B. think we broke our promise."

For the witches, the worst part of this nightmare was the heartbroken face of their best friend. Mr Babbercorn had not looked so pale and sad since the worst days of Mrs Bagg-Meanly. Old Noshie noisily burst into tears.

Skirty Marm looked hard at the curate. "I can see why you don't believe us," she said, "but I wish you could. Me and Nosh would never break a promise we made to you. You're our best human – and we'll carry on liking you, whatever you think of us."

Mr Babbercorn was deeply moved. "I'll always be your friend," he said sadly.

"Me too!" sniffed the vicar.

Skirty Marm turned grandly to PC Bloater. "All right, we're ready. You can put on the nose-irons and the ear-clamps and the leg-cuffs and the itching-belts—"

"Just handcuffs," PC Bloater interrupted. "This isn't your Witch Island."

"I don't like prison!" sobbed Old Noshie. "They make you knit metal underwear for the queen!"

"Silly," Skirty Marm said. "The human queen doesn't wear metal underwear. And her prisons aren't like Mrs Abercrombie's. We'll get a nice little cell."

"Separate cells," said PC Bloater, "to stop you making any more trouble."

"But I want to stay with Skirty!" howled Old Noshie.

"Don't worry, Nosh – I won't leave you!" cried Skirty Marm. She grabbed Old Noshie's hand, and dragged her over to the window. "Brooms!" she shouted. "At the double!"

The two broomsticks lay on the floor under one of the great bells. At the sound of Skirty's voice, they leapt into the air and whizzed across to the witches.

"What do you think you're—" PC Bloater began furiously.

He was too late. To the secret joy of Mr

Babbercorn, who could not bear the idea of his friends in prison, the witches jumped on their broomsticks and dived out of the window.

"Stop crying!" ordered Skirty Marm. "Pay attention."

She steered her broomstick down to the vicarage garden, and landed in some thick laurel bushes. A sobbing Old Noshie crashed down beside her.

"What are we doing here? We should be making our getaway!"

Skirty Marm scowled. "I'm not leaving this village until I've found a way to clear our names. We can't let Mr B. think we told lies. I won't rest until I've unmasked the real culprit!"

"The police will find us!" moaned Old Noshie.

"Not here," Skirty Marm said firmly. "And if they come, we'll make ourselves invisible."

Old Noshie wiped her nose on the brim of her pointed hat and put it back on. Distantly, from the other side of the village, they heard the siren of PC Bloater's borrowed police car. A moment later, the back door of the vicarage banged, telling them that Mr Babbercorn and Mr Snelling had returned home.

Skirty Marm led the way through the bushes to the tumbledown garden shed.

She pushed open the door – and both witches let out great gasps of shock.

"Well, well, well," said Skirty Marm in a voice of simmering fury. "I knew I was right about that cat!"

In a dark corner of the shed sat Tibbles, wearing headphones and mewing into a radio set. They had caught the real culprit – not red-handed, but red-pawed.

4

Mendax

Tibbles gave a strangled "miaow!" and tried to dart past the witches through the open door.

Skirty Marm was too quick for him. She grabbed the cat by the scruff of his neck.

"Oh no, you don't!" she yelled. "You've got some explaining to do, my furry friend! Get the clothes line, Nosh – let's tie him up."

Tibbles struggled and scratched and bit with all his might, but one small cat was no match for two determined witches. In a moment, they had wound him up in the clothes line, until he could not move one of his four paws. He lay on the floor between them, wriggling and spitting.

"I knew it!" raged Skirty Marm. "Didn't I always say this cat was a shady character?"

"You did," agreed Old Noshie. "You were right all along, Skirt."

Skirty picked up the little cat-sized head-

phones Tibbles had been using, and they heard a distant, crackling voice:

"Come in, Agent 400. Are you still receiving us?"

"Oh, it's all clear now!" thundered Skirty Marm. She pointed accusingly at the squirming cat. "This is the VILLAIN who ruined our spells! This is the SCOUNDREL who did all the bad magic in the village! All that pet business was just a cover – he's a SPY!"

Old Noshie's green face was frightened. "But what's a cat-slave doing here? Who's he working for? Oh, Skirty – could it be something to do with the TERRIBLE THING we did to the queen? Is this Mrs Abercrombie's revenge?"

"First things first," said Skirty Marm. "We must show Mr B. and the vicar that we're not wicked after all." She tucked the guilty cat under one ragged arm. "Wait till they see dear little Tibbles in his true colours!"

"Heh, heh!" chuckled Old Noshie, cheering up. "He'll have to give back that fancy duvet now!"

The witches peeped out of the shed, to make sure nobody was watching, then scuttled across the lawn to the vicarage.

Mr Babbercorn and Mr Snelling were feeling very sad because they thought they would never see the escaped witches again. When Old Noshie and Skirty Marm burst in through the kitchen door, their faces lit up with joy.

"My dear witches!" cried Mr Babbercorn. "Thank goodness you're safe! Vicar, couldn't we hide them from the police?"

"It would be very wrong," said Mr Snelling, wiping his eyes, "but I can't bear to turn them over to PC Bloater. We'll put them in the cellar."

Skirty Marm was grinning triumphantly. "You don't have to worry about us any more.

We've found the sneaky, hairy, smelly little SPY who did all that bad magic!"

She whipped the trussed Tibbles out of her rags, and flung him down on the kitchen table.

The vicar and Mr Babbercorn were horrified. As far as they could see, the witches were cruelly hurting an innocent pet cat.

"Really, you've gone too far this time!" spluttered Mr Snelling. "How dare you tie up my Tibbles?"

Mr Babbercorn's pale face was very stern. "What is the meaning of this?"

"This is no ordinary cat!" declared Skirty Marm. "He's a cat-slave, and he's been sent here to SPY on us!"

Tibbles saw the shocked faces of the vicar and the curate. For a fraction of a second, his whiskers twitched with the suspicion of a smirk. Then he stopped wriggling, and gave a feeble, pathetic little mew.

"What nonsense!" cried Mr Snelling. "Tibbles can't even talk – unless you've put a spell on him!"

"Talk!" Old Noshie shouted at Tibbles.

Tibbles mewed again, more pathetically.

Skirty Marm bent over the table, and put her mouth against the cat's ear.

"If you don't talk," she said, "I'll change you into a MOUSE and EAT you." Anyone could see that she meant it.

To the astonishment of Mr Babbercorn and Mr Snelling, Tibbles said, "Don't eat me! There's no need to get hysterical."

His voice was something between a purr and a mew, rather high and breathy but perfectly clear. It made the vicar and the curate feel very strange, to hear it coming from their pet.

"Name and rank?" said Skirty Marm.

"Agent 400," said Tibbles. "I'm a senior officer in the W.I.S.S."

"What on earth is that?" asked Mr Babbercorn, his eyes wide with amazement.

"The Witch Island Secret Service," said Old Noshie. "This is very worrying, Skirty. When we did the TERRIBLE THING, I thought the W.I.S.S. would be closed down."

Tibbles' mouth curved in a proud smirk.

"You have underestimated our Beloved Queen," he purred. "She found an ancient spell to call back the Power Hat – and now she's thirsting for revenge!"

"I'm completely lost," complained Mr Snelling. "What terrible thing? What Power Hat?"

"Tell them, Skirty!" cried Old Noshie.

Skirty Marm was looking more seriously frightened than her friends had ever seen her. "It happened when we flew back to the island, for the potion spell," she said. "We stole the Power Hat and threw it in the sea. We thought that if she didn't have the hat, Mrs A. couldn't be Queen of Witch Island any more. We thought she'd just be an ordinary Purple-Stocking. We thought they'd have to have a proper election."

"Fools!" chortled Tibbles.

Mr Babbercorn sat down. He was bewildered. "I don't understand. What is the Power Hat?"

The witches had never told him about this.

"It's a very magic hat," Old Noshie said in a trembling voice. "It's two metres tall, and it has a candle stuck in the point that never goes out. Nobody really knows everything it can do – but it gives anyone who wears it tremendous magickness."

"If you'd taken the trouble to listen to Witch Island Radio," Tibbles said with a mewing laugh, "on that natty transistor of yours, you'd know what happened after you did that

176

TERRIBLE THING. Yes, there was an election – but Mrs Abercrombie won. She was still the most powerful witch on the island, and the Greens and Purples all voted for her. The Red-Stockings weren't allowed to vote for anyone."

"Typical!" thundered the ex-Red-Stocking Skirty Marm.

"When Mrs A. called back the Power Hat," Tibbles went on, "by summoning her friends the Sea Spirits, it was business as usual on Witch Island."

Old Noshie shivered. "Oh, Skirt! Now we'll never be safe from her!"

Skirty Marm tried to look brave, but she was shivering too. Mrs Abercrombie was a witch of genius, and with the Power Hat back on her hideous head, she was the most dangerous witch in the world. This was the witch who had regularly turned her personal guards into slugs when she got bored with them. And now she was thirsting for revenge!

"So she sent Tibbles to do all that dreadful magic!" said Mr Snelling. "It was very naughty of you, Tibby. How could you let poor Noshie and Skirty take the blame? I've a good mind not to give you any cream for dinner."

"I was only obeying orders," said Tibbles mournfully. "Us cat-slaves must obey the Purple-Stockings. If you untie me, I'll tell you the whole story."

"Don't!" squeaked Old Noshie. "He'll run away!"

Tibbles groaned. "Oh, the PAIN! These ropes cut into my war wound from the Battle of Fungus Gulch!"

Mr Snelling picked up the kitchen scissors, and looked his cat sternly in the eye.

"I'll untie you," he said, "if you promise not to run away."

"I promise!" said Tibbles.

"You'd better keep that promise," hissed Skirty Marm, "or else practise squeaking like a MOUSE!"

The vicar snipped away the clothes line. Tibbles stretched all his paws, smoothed his tail, and sat up on his hind legs.

"Thank you," he said. "You've only heard the witches' side of things so far. I'm afraid the truth will shock you. Old Noshie and Skirty Marm are two extremely dangerous outlaws, wanted on Witch Island for Robbery with Violence."

"He's LYING!" roared the witches.

"Quiet!" ordered Mr Babbercorn. "Go and stand in the corner beside the fridge until he's finished."

Sulkily, the witches went to stand in the corner.

"You humans have been fooled and bamboozled," Tibbles went on. "These witches are the wicked ones. Our Beloved Queen, Mrs Abercrombie, is very sorry for the trouble they've caused. She wanted to spare you the horrible sight of their capture. But if you let me radio for help, she'll send one of her crack broom squadrons, to take them away immediately."

"AARGH!" shrieked Old Noshie.

Skirty Marm was fuming. "It's a pack of LIES!"

"One more interruption," said Mr Babbercorn, "and I'll stuff tea towels in your mouths. Carry on, Tibbles."

Tibbles, turning towards the vicar, made his voice very purry and sweet. "Surely you trust your little Tibby more than a pair of nasty witches?"

The witches gazed at him fearfully. This cat sounded very convincing. What if the humans believed him?

Mr Snelling said, "Old Noshie and Skirty Marm have proved they are our friends. They are brave and noble – and I won't hear a word against them."

"We're proud to know them," added Mr Babbercorn, making the witches' eyes fill with tears of happiness. "Now, suppose you tell us the real truth?"

Tibbles thoughtfully licked a paw. "It's all too true. The queen sent me here to get Old Noshie and Skirty Marm chucked out of this village. I'm her best cat-slave, and I begged her not to do this. 'Your Majesty,' I said, 'it'll only cause trouble with the humans.' But she was too angry to listen. 'Mendax,' she said (that's my real name), 'Mendax – gallant hero of Fungus Gulch – I want these witches CRUSHED, and tell the humans I'll pay for any damage.'"

"What a stinking great load of rubbish!" Skirty Marm said scornfully. "You weren't at the Battle of Fungus Gulch – you're much too young."

"And if you were Mrs Abercrombie's best cat-slave," Old Noshie said, "we'd have seen you combing her beard at the weekly ceremonies!"

"I'm a Secret Agent," said Tibbles-Mendax.

"Naturally, I keep a low profile."

"Pooh," said Skirty Marm. "I don't believe a word of it! The queen would never waste her best cat on a job like this. I bet you're not important at all. Tell us the truth – or start looking for a mouse hole!"

"All right, all right," the cat said with a snarl. "Before I joined the W.I.S.S., I worked in the palace kitchens."

"Har-har-har!" jeered the witches.

"I was very important!" shouted Mendax. "I was the top pastry chef! I trained in witch cuisine, at the Ecole des Sorcières, in Paris!"

Mr Snelling was trying to look serious, but a smile twitched at his lips.

"Mendax is your real name," he said, "and it seems to suit you. In Latin, 'Mendax' means liar."

"You're not on Witch Island now," Mr Babbercorn said kindly. "Don't be afraid of telling us the truth – we won't hurt you."

"I might," muttered Skirty Marm.

"Nobody will hurt you," said Mr Snelling, giving the witches a warning look over the top of his glasses.

Mendax was silent for a whole minute. When

he spoke again, his voice was small and sulky.

"I did work in the palace kitchens – that bit was true. But I wasn't a pastry chef. I belonged to a mean old Purple-Stocking called Mrs Wilkins, who did the washing-up. She never paid me, and never gave me anything nice to eat."

He began to sob. It was moving to see the tears rolling down into his whiskers.

"I washed up in that kitchen until last month, when I was sent to prison for stealing bat cake. They said they'd let me out early if I did a little job for the W.I.S.S. I couldn't refuse! You can't imagine how terrible it is on Witch Island now the queen has got the Power Hat again! The cat-slaves are treated more cruelly than ever. And she's put a freeze on stockings!"

"She's WHAT?" yelled Skirty Marm.

"No promotions for a hundred years," Mendax said. "The Red-Stockings stay Red. The Greens stay Green. And that way, the old Purples keep total power. The Greens are miffed – but the Reds are furious."

"She can't do that!" protested Old Noshie. "She can't stop witches getting older!"

"She can," sniffed Mendax. "She can do

pretty well anything now she's got the Hat. Oh, please, please don't send me back! I never knew how nice humans are until I came here! Mrs Wilkins kicks me and beats me and starves me!"

He knelt on the table and clasped his paws pleadingly.

"If you let me stay here, I'll help with the cooking, I'll play chess with Mr Snelling—"

"Good gracious," interrupted the vicar. "Do you play chess?"

"Do I play!" exclaimed Mendax. "I'm a grand master."

The witches rudely blew raspberries.

"Well, all right," Mendax said, "I don't exactly play chess. But I could learn! And I do play Monopoly. Oh, please let me stay!"

"If I was you," said Skirty Marm, "I'd send this lying, spying little bag of fur straight back to Witch Island!"

"Certainly not," said Mr Snelling. "He can stay with us, and learn to be good. Just as you did."

"Thank you!" cried Mendax, jumping up to lick the vicar's face. "You won't be sorry – I'll be as good as gold! And I'll try ever so hard not to tell any more lies."

Mr Babbercorn noticed that Old Noshie and Skirty Marm still looked suspicious. It was going to take them a while to trust the spy.

"Mendax," he said, "the first thing you must do is tell everyone in this village that the witches are innocent. I will call a parish meeting, and you will make a public confession."

"It'll be the best confession you ever heard," Mendax assured him.

"That's what I'm afraid of," said Mr Babbercorn. "Just make sure it's a true one."

5

Absent Friends

Mendax made his public confession in the village hall. The people of Tranters End were proud of their two local witches, and when they heard that Old Noshie and Skirty Marm were innocent, they burst into loud cheers.

It did not take them long to get used to the vicar's talking cat. In just a few days, they were all saying hello to Mendax when they met him in the street. Everyone liked him because he was extremely polite and obviously trying very hard to behave. He did all the washing-up at the vicarage (except the saucepans which were too heavy for his paws). He cleaned the kitchen floor with a dish mop, which took ages. The vicar gave him a very small shopping basket, and he often popped out to Mrs Tucker's shop. He even baked cakes.

"It's wonderful what he can do with those

little paws," Mr Snelling said happily. "That cat is an absolute treasure."

"Hmmm," said Mr Babbercorn. "I caught him telling the Brownies about how he jumped off the Eiffel Tower for a bet during his student days in Paris. I wish he'd stop those awful lies. Then maybe the witches would trust him."

Old Noshie and Skirty Marm did not join in what Skirty called the "Mendax-mania". They had never liked the cat-slaves – those lackeys of the mean old Purple-Stockings – and still thought Mendax a shady character.

"Once a spy, always a spy!" said Skirty Marm darkly.

She was not pleased to find Mendax waiting in the belfry one afternoon. The witches had been out on their broomsticks, usefully clearing leaves out of the vicarage gutters. They flew in through the window, and there was the small black cat, quivering with excitement.

"At last!" he mewed.

Old Noshie and Skirty Marm looked round suspiciously. Mendax was wearing a small flowery apron. The kettle was boiling, and plates of fresh bats and beetles were laid out neatly on the floor.

The witches were tired and hungry, and could not help feeling rather pleased – though Skirty Marm tried to hide it.

She growled, "What's all this in aid of?"

Mendax, standing on his hind legs with his tail tucked over one arm, poured cups of hot rainwater.

"How do you like your water?" he asked. "One spit, or two?"

"Two," said Old Noshie. "Good, big ones – and a spot of dribble. Thanks, Mendax."

She sat down on her cushion, and watched

Mendax spitting daintily into her tea. It smelled delicious, and she had forgotten to be cross with him.

Skirty Marm, however, was not so easily swayed.

"What are you doing here?"

Mendax passed round the plate of bats. "You've got to let me be your friend. I came here with some very important news."

Skirty Marm snorted rudely. "We're not interested in your big, fat LIES."

"I've given up lying," said Mendax.

"No, you haven't," chuckled Old Noshie with her mouth full. "You told Mrs Tucker you saved the queen's life at Fungus Gulch – what a whopper!"

"I swear, on the vicar's collar, this is true!" cried Mendax. "Oh, witches, please listen! If you care at all about your fellow witches, please trust me! I've had a message for you on my radio set!"

The witches stared. They knew that Mendax still listened to the WBC (Witch Broadcasting Company) on his radio in the garden shed. Could he have picked up a message from the island?

"For us?" gasped Old Noshie.

"It was an SOS," Mendax said, tucking the end of his tail into his apron pocket. "Just a frightened sort of voice – 'Calling Old Noshie and Skirty Marm, wherever you are, help, help, help! You are our only hope!' Then there was a shout, and silence."

This certainly sounded like trouble.

Skirty Marm asked, "Who was it?"

"I don't know," said Mendax, "but I tuned into the news, and heard that some Red-Stocking witches had been plotting against the queen. Two of them disguised themselves as Purples, and were caught breaking into the Palace."

This was sensational. Old Noshie and Skirty Marm had been very shocked to hear about the stocking freeze. They were impressed to hear that their old Red-Stocking friends had not taken the monstrous injustice lying down.

"Most of the plotters escaped," Mendax went on, "but they arrested the ringleader – a witch called Badsleeves."

"BADSLEEVES!" choked Old Noshie. "She had the cave next door to ours! Do you remember, Skirt?"

"Of course," said Skirty Marm. "We shared

many a bat with dear old Baddy. She was just about the only witch I was sorry to leave behind."

Mendax said, "She got caught when her cave-mate went to the police—"

"SNEEVIL!" yelled Skirty Marm in a sudden rage. "That nasty old bag! Didn't I always tell you, Noshie? Steer clear of that Sneevil, I always said. She told bigger lies than this cat, and she STOLE my best BLOOMERS!"

Witch Island is cold and damp, and witches are very serious about their underwear. Stealing these precious garments is considered very low indeed.

"They were a lovely pair," Old Noshie said, "and you'd just got them soft."

Skirty Marm groaned. "This is terrible! There must be something we can do for poor Badsleeves!"

"Her trial is fixed for tonight," said Mendax. "I thought you might like to listen to it on my radio."

"Come on!" Skirty Marm pulled open the door to the one hundred and eighty-six belfry steps. "Let's tell Mr B. He'll know what to do."

*

It took Mr Babbercorn some time to understand the story – partly because he had two witches and a cat all talking at once, and partly because he found the politics of Witch Island so bewildering.

"Your friend Badsleeves sounds very brave," he said when he had grasped the details. "Is there anything you can do to help her?"

"No," sighed Old Noshie. "Not even if we went back to Witch Island."

"And if they went back there," Mendax said, "they'd be thrown into prison at once. They'd never be so daft."

Skirty Marm was frowning her thinking frown. "If we could go back and help Badsleeves to escape, perhaps we could find the other plotters—"

"Are you BONKERS?" screamed Old Noshie, turning the colour of an old sprout. "You'll get us killed!"

"Fat lot of use you'd be, anyway," said Mendax.

Skirty Marm ignored them, and looked at Mr Babbercorn. "I know it'd be dangerous, and I hate dangerous things. But I can't be happy with myself ever again if I don't try

191

to rescue Badsleeves."

Mr Babbercorn patted her ragged, bony shoulder. "You're a noble witch, Skirty."

"I feel just the same," Old Noshie said quickly. She did not, but fancied being called "noble" by the curate. Besides, if Skirty Marm insisted on going into danger, Old Noshie had to go too. Frightened as she was, there was no question of letting her friend go without her.

Mr Babbercorn's eyes were full of tears. "Splendid witches! But should I let you take such a risk?"

Suddenly, Skirty Marm had a terrible thought.

"You!" she turned to Mendax. "You'd better not be lying! Because if this is a trick to get us chucked into prison—"

"It's the truth!" hissed Mendax. "And to prove it, I'll go back to Witch Island with you!"

The witches were thunderstruck.

"But you're a cat-slave!" said Old Noshie. "If you get caught, they'll use you as a brush for cleaning chimneys!"

Mendax looked proud. "I'm tired of you all thinking I can't be trusted. As a matter of fact, I hate Mrs Abercrombie's government as much as you do. You'll find it pretty useful, having a cat-slave on your side."

"All right," growled Skirty Marm, "you can come with us. But no funny business – or else!"

"Or else we'll biff you right into next week," said Old Noshie.

Mendax jumped off the top of the television set, and went towards the kitchen.

"I'll make some sandwiches for the journey."

The short winter's day was nearly over when Old Noshie and Skirty Marm prepared to mount their broomsticks in the vicarage garden. Mr Babbercorn had given them each a pair of his own long woolly pants to keep out the bitter cold. The witches found them superbly comfortable, and wonderfully elegant.

"They're almost as good as my stolen bloomers," Skirty Marm said.

They looked rather funny, sticking out underneath the witches' black rags, but the vicar and the curate felt far too anxious to laugh.

"Good luck," said Mr Babbercorn. "Try to stay out of trouble. Obviously, you must use as much magic as you like. Anything, to save your poor friend and bring justice to Witch Island."

Mendax sat in a basket on the back of Old Noshie's broom, with the smallest saucepan tied on his head as a crash helmet.

"If I don't come back," he said bravely, "please give my duvet to the cat at the post office."

Soft-hearted Mr Snelling was weeping. "Do be careful! I'll miss you all so dreadfully!"

It was a long and difficult ride to Witch Island. Old Noshie and Skirty Marm put on their goggles and muttered the revving-up spell to start their brooms. Skirty Marm checked the

switches on the broom handles, which enabled them to talk to each other while flying.

"Contact!" she cried. "Set course for W.I.!" And the two brooms zoomed off into the darkening sky.

The night was freezing, and the cold became mixed with a terrible dampness as they approached Witch Island. The old home of the witches and Mendax looked very black and bleak when the two brooms landed on the sooty palace beach. The air was damp and chilly with sea spray, and smelled of bad eggs.

"So far, so good," said Skirty Marm. "Not a soul about. They must all be packed into the Meeting Cave."

"Let's have our sandwiches," suggested Old Noshie. She stuffed a mouse roll into her mouth.

"Put those away!" snapped Skirty Marm. "We need to find a way into that Meeting Cave without being seen."

"That's impossible!" cried Old Noshie. "And I refuse to be killed and stuffed and put in the queen's trophy room, until I've finished my picnic!"

"Quiet," said Skirty Marm. "I'm thinking."

She wriggled her fingers and toes. The smelly

air of her old home made her tingle with inspiration.

"Of course!" she said. "Mendax, you're a cat-slave. You can sneak us in through the cats' alley!"

Mendax had gone very quiet. He was trembling, from the ends of his whiskers to the tip of his tail.

"I was afraid you'd think of that," he said. He took off his saucepan helmet. "You'd better follow me. Leave the brooms under this big rock. And the sandwiches."

"Drat," grumbled Old Noshie. "I'm starving!"

They hid the broomsticks and sandwiches. Putting his paw to his mouth, Mendax led the witches through a hidden opening in the massive black rock, and into a dark, winding tunnel. It was one of the tunnels built specially for cat-slaves, and very cramped. Old Noshie and Skirty Marm had to crawl on their hands and knees.

"Ow!" complained Old Noshie, who was rather plump, "My bottom keeps getting stuck! And these rocks will wear out our new long johns."

"Shhh!" hissed Skirty Marm. "Or some

stinky cat-slave will hear us and give us away to the Purples!"

"No offence, Mendax," said Old Noshie.

"Hmph!" snorted Skirty Marm. She was annoyed that her friend found it so easy to be nice to the spy.

The crawl along the cats' alley was very uncomfortable, and seemed to take ages. At last, they saw a light at the tunnel's end. It grew brighter, and suddenly the two witches found themselves peering through a small opening, high up in the wall of the Meeting Cave.

"Wow!" gasped Old Noshie.

It was an incredible sight. The huge Meeting Cave was seething with every witch on the island – from ancient Purple-Stockings of five and six hundred years old, to baby Yellows of only seventy or eighty. On the high platform stood the enormous granite throne of Mrs Abercrombie. The stone walls echoes with the shrieks and shouts of thousands of witches fighting for the best seats.

A public trial was a great event on Witch Island, and everyone was in a holiday mood. Around the feet of the crowd ran dozens of cat-slaves with trays of snacks and drinks.

"The lower class of cat," whispered Mendax. "They belong to the Purples who have food licences, poor creatures."

Old Noshie and Skirty Marm were not interested in the cat-slaves. They were staring down at their old comrades, the Red-Stockings. These young witches – all under suspicion because of the plot – sat in a special section of the cave, looking very sulky, and surrounded by police witches.

"They all hate the stocking freeze," Skirty Marm said. "It's all right for the Greens – they have enough power to keep them satisfied. But who wants to stay a Red with smelly old Greens and Purples telling you what to do? It's a scandal! It's an insult! Shall the Red-Stockings accept defeat? No!"

"Stop making speeches!" Old Noshie whispered crossly. "What are we going to do now?"

They were in terrible danger. As soon as one of the busy witches below them thought of looking up, they would be discovered and arrested.

"Well, it's impossible," said Old Noshie. "Let's go home."

Skirty Marm, fingers crossed, mumbled a spell.

"Help!" squealed Old Noshie. "I feel funny . . . something's happening to my legs . . ."

Her voice trailed off into a long miaow. Her black rags and new long johns turned into black, silky fur. Before her astonished eyes, her hands and feet changed into paws.

"Good gracious!" said Mendax.

"I don't like it!" mewed the cat who was Old Noshie. "We'll get trodden on!"

"Now you know how it feels to be a helpless slave," said Mendax.

Skirty Marm picked up her new tail and gazed at it, fascinated. "I don't know what you lot find to compain about. This feels great."

"Just wait!" Mendax said darkly. "Wait till some old Purple kicks you with her smelly fat foot and sends you off to work in the sulphur mines!"

"Blimey," muttered Old Noshie, "aren't these whiskers itchy?"

Now that they were cats, they could easily run down the narrow ledge of rock, to the heart of the Meeting Cave. As Skirty Marm had hoped, none of the excited witches took any notice of three more cat-slaves.

"But we've got to get proper disguises, before someone notices we don't belong to anyone," said Mendax. "Come on – I'll show you how to behave. I don't suppose either of you know a decent sleeping spell?"

"No!" quavered Old Noshie. "Let's go home!"

"Shut up, you coward!" mewed Skirty Marm. Red sparks flew from the ends of her whiskers. "Of course I know a sleeping spell! Get on with it, Mendax – and less of your cheek!"

She did not like taking orders from a cat, but knew that she had no choice. The two friends followed Mendax through a small, cat-sized door in the mossy wall of the cave. Behind it, they found three cat-slaves, refilling their trays of food and drink from a large box. An ugly Purple-Stocking stood over them with a cat whip.

"Hurry up!" she growled. "Move those paws!"

Skirty Marm mumbled the sleeping spell (always one of her best). The Purple-Stocking witch and her three cat-slaves instantly fell into a deep sleep.

"Right," said Mendax over the snores of the

Purple. "Stand up on your back legs, put the trays round your necks, do what I do . . . and don't be too polite to the Red-Stockings."

Old Noshie and Skirty Marm put on their trays – with some difficulty, because they were not used to having paws instead of hands. Mendax had to show Old Noshie how to put her tail over one arm so it would not trip her up. At last, their disguise was complete.

Mendax strolled back into the Meeting Cave, mewing at the top of his voice, "Pond sludge! Fried weasel! Newt skulls! Get your snacks here!"

"Snacks!" mewed the witches bravely. "Get your lovely snacks here!"

It was awful to be so small among so many fierce Purple- and Green-Stockings. Old Noshie and Skirty Marm did not dare to look around, but kept their eyes fixed on Mendax's back.

"Oi! Cat!" yelled a nasty voice. A wrinkled hand shot out of the crowd and grabbed Mendax by the ear. It belonged to a Green-Stocking. "Fried weasel – and be quick about it!"

Mendax handed over a weasel, and took the Green-Stocking's money.

"Tut tut," he said. "Haven't you got the right change?"

"None of your lip!" screamed the Green-Stocking. "Don't you see the colour of these stockings?"

Skirty Marm glanced up at the witch's face, and let out a sudden spit of fury.

"Look!" she whispered to the cat who was Old Noshie, "That's no Green! It's SNEEVIL! The queen must have promoted her as a reward for betraying Badsleeves! Oh, wouldn't I love to squash her nose?"

Old Noshie gulped. The Green-Stocking was indeed the wicked Sneevil who had once shared the cave next to theirs.

Skirty Marm dropped to the floor, just long enough to look up Sneevil's dress.

"I knew it!" she hissed. "She's wearing them!"

"Shut up about your bloomers," groaned Old Noshie, "or you'll ruin everything!"

Mendax had counted out Sneevil's change. He nodded to the witches, and they followed him through the crowd. Several times, witches stopped them to buy snacks. Old Noshie and Skirty Marm were very shocked by the rude way the older witches spoke to cat-slaves. After twenty minutes, their sides were black and blue from kicks and pinches.

"I know," said Mendax, seeing their faces. "You're not the only ones who want a revolution."

He settled them inside a dip in the cave wall, with a beautiful view of the platform. They were just a few metres above the dock, where Badsleeves would soon be standing. They could not forget that they had once stood there themselves, on the terrible day of their trial for singing the rude song about Mrs Abercrombie.

"Poor Badsleeves," said Old Noshie, "I know how she must be feeling."

Suddenly, there was a deafening fanfare of trumpets.

"Look out," said Skirty Marm. "Here comes Mrs Stinkbomb, our glorious queen."

6

S.L.A.W.

A great silence fell upon the Meeting Cave. Two ceremonial cat-slaves, wearing collars of gold, marched onto the platform and stood on either side of the massive stone throne.

In stomped the Queen of all the Witches, Mrs Abercrombie. Her red eyes glittered meanly in her ugly face. Her iron teeth gleamed, and her grey beard shot out sparks of fury. Her gigantic body dropped down on the throne, with a mighty "plop".

Every witch in the cave – including the sulky Red-Stockings – bowed until their noses touched the floor. They were all terrified of Mrs Abercrombie. Upon her horrible head, she wore the Power Hat. It was as black and gleaming as a piece of coal, and it stood two metres high. The everlasting candle in its point burned with a bright white stillness.

This was the magic hat Skirty Marm had thrown into the sea, thinking it would end the Queen's cruel reign. She had not known that Mrs Abercrombie's magic would be strong enough to call it back. Was there any place on earth that her magic could not reach? Without the hat, she was brilliant. With it, she was invincible.

"BRING IN THE PRISONER!" she thundered, in a voice that made the walls vibrate.

Old Noshie and Skirty Marm looked down from their hiding place above the dock, impatient to see Badsleeves. Instead, to their surprise, they saw only a police witch carrying a jam jar. The jam jar was filled with greenish water.

"I was too ANGRY to sit through a whole trial," roared Mrs Abercrombie. "I am going to find her guilty anyway – so why waste time?"

She pointed a meaty, accusing finger at the jam jar.

"My subjects, behold the criminal, BADSLEEVES – or what's left of her. I've turned her into a little piece of pond slime. And let this be a warning to all who plot against my sacred person!"

"WOE!" yelled all the witches. "WOE to the TRAITOR!"

The applause crashed on for several minutes. The witches cheered and whistled and stamped their feet. The baby Yellow-Stockings waved black flags and hideous photographs of their queen. The police witches watched the Red-Stockings to make sure they clapped hard enough.

Mrs Abercrombie (with a satisfied smirk that did not improve her face) signalled for silence.

"Badsleeves will have plenty of time to accept my government. I have sentenced her to FIVE HUNDRED YEARS at the bottom of the palace pond."

"Hurrah! Hurrah!" cheered all the witches. "Long live Mrs Abercrombie!"

The queen's hairy face blackened in a disgusting scowl.

"And you cocky little Red-Stockings – so pleased with yourselves for opposing ME – since you fancy yourselves so much, you can stay Red-Stockings until I get my temper back!"

A great groan of outrage went up from the Red-Stockings.

"Well, that's that," sighed Old Noshie. "There's nothing we can do for poor Badsleeves now. Let's go home."

The words were hardly out of her mouth

when the Meeting Cave was suddenly rocked by a tremendous explosion. A cloud of bright red smoke billowed up from the floor, filling the whole cave with scarlet fog.

In the second of horrified silence that followed, a voice shouted, "Justice for Red-Stockings! Down with the government!"

The cave erupted in confusion and pandemonium. As the fog spread, witches screamed and coughed, and surged towards the exits. Mrs Abercrombie was rushed away through a trap-door in the platform by her hand-picked guard of beefy Purples.

Old Noshie and Skirty Marm stared, open-mouthed, until Mendax nudged them hard.

"Quick!" he mewed above the din. "Now's your chance!"

Seeing at once what he meant, the two disguised witches leapt down into the dock. Skirty Marm gabbled a spell that turned them both back into witches. Old Noshie biffed the police witch, who was too shocked to defend herself. Skirty Marm grabbed the jar of pond slime that was Badsleeves.

Just as she was gazing wildly around, wondering what on earth to do next, she felt the paws of Mendax landing on her shoulder.

"The door!" he purred against her ear. "Through the door! I know a way out!"

There was a door at the back of the dock, which led to a bare corridor (Skirty and Noshie dimly remembered being led down it, in handcuffs, on the day of their own trial). The witches and Mendax dived through this door, and dashed off down the corridor. Three fierce police witches dashed after them. Noshie and Skirty biffed right and left, until two of the police witches lay stunned at their feet with their hats pulled down over their faces.

"Nice work, Nosh!" shouted Skirty Marm.

Mendax was sitting on the head of the third police witch. He bit her ear, and she ran away down the corridor, blowing her whistle for help.

A second later, the corridor echoed with the sound of approaching police boots.

Old Noshie flew into a panic, and grabbed the back of Skirty Marm's ragged black dress. A large part of it ripped away in her hand, and Skirty reacted by biffing her friend's nose.

"You clumsy moron!" she shouted. "I've been working on these rags for years!"

"I couldn't help it!" roared Old Noshie.

Round the bend in the corridor, voices bellowed, "Stop! In the name of the queen!"

Unlike the witches, Mendax had stayed calm. He was feeling along the wall, near the floor. His clever paws pressed something, and a section of the wall swung open. The door was very small, but there was no time for Noshie and Skirty to change themselves back into cats. They dived through the small door, and it clanged shut behind them.

They were suddenly in total silence and total darkness. Skirty Marm lit the end of her finger (witches can easily do this without hurting themselves) and held up the flame. Its reflection shone dully on the close, damp walls.

"Where are we?" she asked.

Mendax's eyes gleamed like emeralds in the eerie light.

"I've let you into a secret cat tunnel," he said. "The island's full of them, but this is the first time a witch has ever been inside. If the other cats get to hear about this, I'll be thrown to the sharks."

Skirty Marm cleared her throat. She hated apologizing, but this needed to be said.

"Mendax, I'm sorry I've been horrid to you.

You saved our lives just now. You are on our side, after all. Please forgive me for not trusting you."

Mendax beamed happily. "Don't mention it. After all, we didn't meet in the best circumstances." He held out his paw, and the witches both shook it.

Skirty Marm checked the jam jar.

"You saved Badsleeves, too," she said, peering into the greenish water. "I hope we haven't spilled her."

"Can you change her back, Skirt?" Old Noshie asked anxiously.

Skirty Marm did not like admitting there were things she could not do, but she had to shake her head. "This spell is far too tough for me to budge. It would take a Purple-Stocking, at least."

"I wonder if she can hear us in there?" said Old Noshie. She leaned closer to the jar. "Hello, Baddy. It's Old Noshie – remember me? We're being chased by the police and we'll probably end up getting killed, but we don't want you to worry."

"Fat lot of comfort you are!" Skirty Marm said scornfully. She was still very angry about her torn rags. She shone her flaming finger around the blackness. "I wish I knew where we were. Mendax, where does this secret tunnel of yours come out?"

Mendax wrinkled his nose. "The sewers."

The witches cried, "Oh, BLEUCHH!"

Few sewers are pleasant places, but the sewers of Witch Island are more disgusting than you can possibly imagine. Even the most hardened old Purples, who usually like a bit of filth, refuse to go down there. All maintenance work is carried out by cat-slaves who don't have any choice.

"Well, that's done it," said Skirty Marm. Her voice was gloomy. "There are hundreds of miles of sewers. We could be lost in here for years."

"Ahem," said Mendax. He looked unhappy. "I happen to know my way around."

"This is no time for one of your lies!" snapped Old Noshie.

Mendax sighed. "I'm not lying. I used to work in the sewers when Mrs Wilkins was Effluent Manager."

The witches gasped. A sewer was the last place you would expect to find an elegant cat like Mendax.

"You said she worked in the palace kitchen . . ." faltered Old Noshie.

"She did – afterwards," Mendax said with a shudder. "Believe it or not, washing dishes was regarded as a promotion. To be honest, I preferred the sewers. I didn't have to see so much of Mrs Wilkins."

Old Noshie stroked his smooth back kindly. "Poor Mendax, you had a horrid life on this island."

His green eyes flooded with tears. "You cannot imagine," he said, "the degradation of being the cat-slave of a low-class Purple like Mrs Wilkins. Can you wonder that I dislike the truth?" He shuddered again. "She won me in a game of ping-pong when I was a kitten. She kicked me, she starved me – she got drunk and sent me down to the Nasty Medicine shop with the empties. A cat of my calibre . . . But enough of this." Mendax coughed, and proudly raised his head. "Let us proceed."

On their hands and knees, Old Noshie and Skirty Marm began to crawl along the secret tunnel. It was hard, unpleasant work. Skirty Marm held up her lighted finger. Old Noshie carried the jam jar very carefully, sometimes

saying a comforting word or two to Badsleeves.

At last, after nearly an hour of this, the cat tunnel stopped short at a stone door.

"This will take us into the main sewer," said Mendax. "There's a lot of gas down there, and we don't want another explosion. You'd better put out that finger."

"Not to worry, Badsleeves," Old Noshie told the jar. "Your pond water will get calmer in a minute, when I can stand up."

Skirty Marm blew out the flame at the tip of her finger. For a moment, they were plunged back into blackness. Then the low door opened and they emerged into a far bigger tunnel – dim and dripping, with a thick stream oozing between the brick banks. The smell was amazingly disgusting. Mendax's eyes watered, and he staggered backwards.

"Bit whiffy in here," remarked Old Noshie.

"It is rather strong," agreed Skirty Marm.

There was a cramped stone path beside the sluggish stream. Every twenty metres or so it widened into a deep bay. The faint, sickly light came from lamps set into the slimy walls.

"I think—" began Mendax.

Nobody ever knew what he thought. Before he could finish the sentence, something grabbed him from behind and clamped a dirty hand across his mouth.

At the same moment two witches, their faces hidden by black masks, jumped on Old Noshie and Skirty Marm.

It is difficult to know where you are going, when your hands are tied and you are wearing a blindfold. By the time the masked witches had stopped pulling and shoving, Noshie and Skirty were exhausted.

Rough hands pushed them down on a hard, cold floor.

A stern voice growled, "Take off their blindfolds!"

The blindfolds were untied, and Old Noshie and Skirty Marm blinked as they gazed around. They seemed to be in one of the deep brick bays beside the main sewer. The shadows were studded with dozens of pairs of gleaming eyes. Skirty Marm looked from the eyes down to the legs below. In the dim light, she saw something that made her break into a broad smile.

"You're Red-Stockings!" she shouted. "Oh, this is just like old times! What are you doing down here?"

"We ask the questions," growled the voice. "Who are you working for?"

"The police, I bet," someone said. "I vote we give them a good bashing."

"Well, I'll be blowed," said Skirty Marm, staring hard at the first speaker. "It's Binbag!"

And the Red-Stocking called Binbag gasped, "Blimey, it's Skirty Marm! And the other's Old Noshie – I'd know that vacant green face anywhere!"

This caused a sensation. There were shouts

and cheers. Noshie and Skirty were untied, and thirty beaming witches tried to shake their hands and slap them on the back.

Binbag had been at school with Old Noshie and Skirty Marm, and a great grin was plastered across her toothless face.

"Our heroines!" she cried. "You heard our radio message, and you came to help us!"

"Oh, that was you, was it?" said Old Noshie. She had made up her mind to be very cross about being kidnapped, but couldn't help liking the word "heroines".

Binbag swelled importantly. "This is our secret hideout. We are the S.L.A.W." She added, "That stands for the Secret Liberation Army of Witches. We were going to call ourselves Red-Stockings Against the Stocking Freeze, but that didn't make such a nice word. It was us who hatched that plot against Mrs Abercrombie – and us who made that lovely explosion at the trial. Now we're outlaws, and the whole island is looking for us. That's why we have to hide down here." She stood up. "But we will never surrender! We're going to knock Mrs A. off her throne, once and for all!"

She began to sing:

"Witches arise, at the break of the dawn!
March to the celebration!
Make Mrs A. wish she'd never been born,
O Army of Witch Liberation!"

One by one, the other witches took up the song, until the whole sewer rang with it.

"Spirits of Noshie and Skirty Marm,
Inspire us in our endeavour!
Biff them and bash them – but keep us from harm,
You who are so bold and clever!"

"There's twenty-three more verses," said Binbag.

"I liked the bit about us," said Old Noshie, who was not often called "clever".

"You two are legends among us Red-Stockings," Binbag told her. "When you were first banished, we thought you were dead. Then you came back and chucked the Power Hat into the sea. Now we need your help again."

"Wait!" Skirty Marm cried suddenly. "Where's Mendax?"

"Who? Oh, you mean that cat." Binbag

pointed to a sack on the floor. It was squirming and uttering stifled mews.

Noshie and Skirty rushed to let Mendax out and untie his gag. They had forgotten him because they had been too busy basking in compliments, and now they felt very guilty.

"You beasts!" said Old Noshie. "You've rumpled his whiskers!"

All the other witches had shrunk back against the slimy wall. As far as they knew, all cat-slaves were the tools of the enemy. Skirty Marm saw that she had to introduce this particular cat properly.

"Listen, you lot," she said. "This is Mendax, and he's a friend of ours. He saved our lives today. He showed us that the cat-slaves are only mean to us because the oldies treat them so badly. They want to be free. We won't help your S.L.A.W. unless you promise to free the cat-slaves!"

"Hear! hear," said Mendax, smoothing his squashed whiskers.

"I suppose so," Binbag said doubtfully. "If they all promise to vote for Badsleeves when we have our first election."

"Badsleeves!" choked Old Noshie and Skirty

Marm, suddenly remembering the jar of pond slime.

"Oh dear," said Mendax.

"She was in that jam jar," whispered Old Noshie. "Did you happen to save it?"

To her great surprise, the S.L.A.W. witches giggled.

"It fell in the water," said Binbag. The other witches giggled harder.

"You old fools!" yelled Skirty Marm. "You've just thrown your leader into the sewer!"

"Hello, Skirt," said a familiar voice. "Hello, Noshie."

To the amazement of Old Noshie and Skirty Marm, out of the shadows stepped their old friend and neighbour, Badsleeves. She was a short, stout witch, with sticking-up white hair and round glasses. She chuckled, when she saw their shocked faces.

"Binbag stole an Advanced Purple Spell-book," she explained. "I was smuggled out of prison on the bottom of her shoe, and she changed me back into a witch just before the trial. There was nothing in that jam jar of yours except ordinary pond slime. From a pond."

"Huh," Old Noshie muttered crossly. "I

needn't have tried to cheer it up!"

"Sorry, Noshie," said Badsleeves. "It was really kind of you." She gazed at them solemnly, through her little round glasses. "And I'm afraid I have to ask you to do something else for us."

Old Noshie and Skirty Marm, remembering that they were legends and heroines with a song about them, cried, "Anything!"

"All of us in this sewer are marked witches," said Badsleeves. "The minute we show ourselves, we'll be arrested. But nobody knows you two are on the island. That means you won't show up on the queen's radar. So we need you to

221

sneak past the palace guards, and steal back the Power Hat."

The two Legends squealed.

"Oh, that's ALL, is it?" shouted Skirty Marm sarcastically. "ALL we have to do is steal the Power Hat? Well, pooh to you – you always were a BARMY sort of witch."

"I bet the queen never takes that hat off for a single minute," said Old Noshie. "Not after last time. I bet she's guarded round the clock. We wouldn't stand a chance!"

"True," said Badsleeves. "The Hat is heavily guarded at all times."

Skirty Marm was unhappy. She did not enjoy disappointing her fans by letting S.L.A.W. down.

"We'd help you if there was any way at all," she said. "But don't you see? It's IMPOSSIBLE!"

"Ahem," said Mendax.

Everyone turned to look at him. He coolly licked his paw.

"May I make a suggestion?"

7

A Good Clean Fight

"Here is the problem," Mendax said. "If you don't knock Mrs Abercrombie off her throne, you lot will have to hide in the sewers for ever. You can't get rid of Mrs Abercrombie, unless you get hold of the Power Hat. And you'll never get the Power Hat unless you can sneak past her guards."

All the witches nodded sadly. It looked hopeless.

"But there is a chance," the intelligent cat went on. "There is one time of day when the queen is totally ALONE. And that is when—"

"When she takes her BATH!" interrupted Badsleeves. "Don't be ridiculous, cat. How are we supposed to sneak into the queen's bathroom? Why, she has ten of her biggest, meanest guards outside the door!"

"It'll be risky," Mendax said, "but I'm sure

it can be done. Listen . . ."

Quietly and calmly, he outlined his bold plan. Old Noshie and Skirty Marm were horrified as they heard what they were supposed to do – apart from anything else, the idea of Mrs Abercrombie without any clothes on made them feel quite faint. But the S.L.A.W. were relying on them, and they could not let their friends down now.

"Very well," said Badsleeves when Mendax had finished. "If you can do the dangerous part, we'll do the rest."

She shook hands with Old Noshie and Skirty Marm, and also shook the paw of Mendax.

"Goodbye," she said. "And thank you. Witch Island will never forget your courage."

"I may write another verse about you for our song," piped up Binbag. "So goodbye, and don't worry that it's all been for nothing."

"Why do you keep saying goodbye?" Old Noshie demanded crossly. "Don't you want to see us again?"

There was an embarrassed silence.

"Of course, we want to see you again," said Badsleeves. "It's just that we probably won't."

"I hope it's not too painful," said Binbag.

"Look on the bright side. She might do it quickly."

"Remember!" cried Badsleeves. "You'll be making history! Your glorious names will live for ever!"

"Hmm," muttered Skirty Marm, "I'd just like my glorious body to live until tomorrow, thanks."

Binbag slapped her on the back. "When it's all over, we'll give you a lovely funeral— I mean, party."

Not surprisingly, when Old Noshie and Skirty Marm set off along the sewer on their mission, they were very depressed.

"Well, this is a nice mess," said Skirty Marm.

"Mr Babbercorn will miss us," sniffed Old Noshie.

"Brace up, witches!" said Mendax. "I remember at Fungus Gulch, when I was about to lead my lads in that last, desperate attack on Bendy Ridge—"

"SHUT UP!" roared both the witches.

"Sorry," sighed Mendax. "I was only lying to keep my spirits up."

Mendax was leading, for they were headed for the palace kitchens where he had once worked. There was a cat-slaves' alley joining it to the sewers. Once again, Old Noshie and Skirty Marm had to squeeze themselves through a damp, narrow tunnel. By now, their elbows were covered in grazes and their black rags had run into dozens of new holes. Curiously, however, the long johns given by Mr Babbercorn remained as good as new.

"If a witch got herself a few pairs of these and sold them on this island," Skirty Marm said, "she'd make her fortune."

"Here we are," whispered Mendax. He was trembling all over. "Oh, what ghastly memories come surging back! What endless nights of whipping and biffing!"

From the other side of the cats' door, Old Noshie and Skirty Marm heard the sounds of the busy kitchen – pans clanking, crockery rattling, loud voices and running footsteps. Mrs Abercrombie's appetite was huge, and so were the appetites of her hand-picked guards. The palace kitchens were never idle.

Mendax curled himself round Old Noshie's neck like a black scarf, and hid under her rags.

He whispered ticklish instructions into her ear. "Open the door . . . keep your heads down . . . turn right at the cupboard marked 'Overalls' . . ."

The two witches obeyed him, with their hearts in their mouths. It was ghastly to plunge into a huge, smoky, steamy kitchen full of dangerous old Greens and Purples. On one side of the room was a great fire, where chefs and cat-slaves worked around bubbling cauldrons, stirring, frying and basting. Cat-slaves with trays tied to their backs ran to and fro with stacks of dirty plates.

"The Bath Snack is being prepared," whispered Mendax. "One trolley for the queen, and five for the guardroom. Get yourselves some overalls, for goodness' sake."

The overall cupboard was covered with notices. "Protective Clothing to be Worn at All Times." "No Singing." "Do Not Kill Cat-Slaves near Royal Food." Doing their best to look casual, Old Noshie and Skirty Marm put on big white aprons and tall white hats. Old Noshie pulled her hat down low, to hide her green face.

"That's the one," whispered Mendax. "The huge trolley near the sink."

The sink was the size of a small swimming pool. A crowd of cat-slaves were busily washing dishes around it. Their fur was soaking wet and covered with blobs of old food. Their paws were cracked and swollen.

This was where Mendax had worked. Old Noshie heard a sob in her ear, and wished she dared to say something comforting. She and Skirty Marm had never dreamed that the mysterious cat-slaves could be treated so cruelly.

A truly revolting old Purple-Stocking, reeking of Nasty Medicine, stood over the sink with a cat whip. Every few minutes, she shouted, "Faster!" and brought her whip down on a cat's back.

"That's Mrs Wilkins," whispered Mendax. "Drunk, as usual."

"Smelly old beast!" Skirty Marm said in a kind of whispered growl. "Don't worry, Mendax – we'll set your friends free. I'm so angry now, I'm not even scared!"

"Well, I'm terrified," said Old Noshie. "I'm so terrified that my tummy keeps gurgling."

The queen's snack trolley was enormous, and heaped with covered dishes. It wafted out a strong smell of baked bat, which made Old Noshie's stomach gurgle worse than ever. A bell rang so loudly that the big saucepans on the walls shook like the church bells of Tranters End. Two large Green-Stocking under-chefs kicked their way through the cat-slaves, and pushed the Royal trolley out of the kitchen.

"Go on!" hissed Mendax. "You've got five minutes before the other trolleys leave!"

Very scared, Old Noshie and Skirty Marm scuttled after the queen's Bath Snack. Skirty Marm managed to pick up a heavy ladle without being noticed by the bustling kitchen witches.

"Don't biff until you see the reds of their eyes!" she whispered.

Skirty Marm rather liked a good fight. Old

Noshie did not, and she was shaking like a jelly.

"This is crazy!" she squeaked. "They're HUGE!"

The rocky corridor outside the kitchen was deserted. It was now or never – this was the window of opportunity upon which Mendax had based his plan. He tightened his paws round Old Noshie's neck. Skirty Marm swung her ladle, and dealt the biggest trolley witch a handsome wallop. Old Noshie jumped at the other one, but was not fast enough. The angry Green-Stocking pulled a switch in the stone wall.

"Whoops," said Mendax.

A door opened in the wall. There was a rushing sound, and out zoomed two armoured broomsticks without riders.

"You're finished!" screamed one of the Green-Stockings. "You're going straight to prison!"

"No, we're not!" cried Skirty Marm. To Old Noshie's surprise, she held up her hand, and shouted, "Brooms! Set 'em off, brooms!"

To Noshie's greater surprise, the two armoured broomsticks suddenly changed direction and jumped on the two Green-Stockings. Automatic handcuffs shot out of their brushes. In a very few minutes, they had cuffed the two roaring, spitting Greens and bundled them through a very smelly flap in the wall near by.

"The rubbish chute," said Mendax with a purr of satisfaction. "How very appropriate."

"But how?" gasped Old Noshie.

"Don't you recognize them?" Skirty Marm chuckled. "Our old brooms! The ones who left us when we got to Tranters End! They've been retrained – but they haven't forgotten us!" She patted both broomsticks. "Thanks, brooms. As you were."

The two broomsticks glided serenely away.

"Quick!" mewed Mendax.

Old Noshie whipped the cover off one of the dishes on the trolley – a selection of cold bats, mice and porcupines. Mendax jumped onto the plate.

"Cor," said Old Noshie, "doesn't it smell lovely?"

She replaced the cover. Now it was time for the hardest part. The witches began to push the trolley towards the Royal bathroom.

A very big Purple-Stocking – one of Mrs Abercrombie's elite guards – stood outside the entrance to the queen's private suite.

Skirty Marm and Old Noshie were trembling with terror when they pushed the trolley past her. But all she said was, "Hurry up with those snacks – she's in a horrible temper."

Echoing through the underground caves, a dreadful voice bellowed, "WHERE'S MY SNACK?"

Only a few metres to the bathroom – but it was the longest walk of the witches' lives. Never had their belfry seemed so safe and cosy. Keeping their heads well down, they had to push the trolley through the outer room full of guards. The red badges on the guards' pointed hats marked them out as the most vicious witches on the island.

One of them pushed open the door to the queen's bathroom.

"ABOUT TIME!" grumbled Mrs Abercrombie. "Keep me waiting again, and it's SEWER DUTY for the lot of you!"

The bathroom was full of steam. Through the damp clouds they could make out a huge stone bath. In this, the Queen of the Witches lay, like a great, wobbly whale. Her mottled purple body was naked except for her Power Hat. The everlasting candle in its point gleamed through the steam with a cold, white radiance. Mrs Abercrombie was scrubbing under her arms with a soapy hedgehog.

"I'll start with a dish of sugared newts," she said.

Old Noshie and Skirty Marm picked up the largest dish, carried it between them to the edge of the bath, and took off the cover.

"AARGH!" bellowed Mrs Abercrombie.

Mendax leapt out like a streak of black lightning, and sank his claws into the Power

Hat. The queen pulled him off and threw him into the water. This gave the two witches just enough time to grab at the Power Hat and wrap their arms around it. It tingled and fizzed with magic.

"GUARDS!" roared Mrs Abercrombie.

Noshie and Skirty pulled with all their might. The Hat was stuck firmly to the Royal head – but Skirty Marm's great anger gave her strength. With a mighty effort, she managed to prise it off. It toppled into the deep, murky water where poor Mendax was struggling to keep his nose above the surface.

"Don't – let – her – get – it – back!" he gasped.

Four guards burst into the bathroom.

"Don't just stand there!" shouted the queen. "Call this security? You're all fired!"

Dropping the hedgehog, she pointed a finger each at Old Noshie and Skirty Marm, and spat out a spell.

At that moment, the witches gave themselves up for lost and prepared to be turned into slugs, pond slime, or another of the queen's favourite punishments.

But nothing happened. The four guards screamed. Old Noshie and Skirty Marm gaped in astonishment. Never before had one of the queen's spells failed.

"Drat," swore Mrs Abercrombie. "They're under some kind of protection and I can't shift it!" She peered through the steam. "It's those long pants. Get them off."

"Mr Babbercorn's long johns!" cried Skirty Marm. "Don't you see, Nosh? They've been worn by a human curate, and now she can't touch us!"

"We'll see about that!" snarled Mrs Abercrombie. The Power Hat lay at the bottom of the bath, beside the queen's mighty behind. Its everlasting candle gleaming eerily under the water. The queen popped a bar of soap into her mouth, and made a grab for the Hat. "I don't care if all your underwear belongs to the Archbishop of Canterbury – it's powerless against my Hat!"

Mendax was too quick for her. He drew a deep breath, and dived under the water. When Mrs Abercrombie pulled the Power Hat out of the water, she gave her first scream of real fear – the little cat had crawled inside it, and was clinging to it like a burr. The furious queen shook it and banged it against the wall, but she could not dislodge him.

Now there were three witches and a cat in the bath, punching and swiping and sending up great fountains of water.

Noshie and Skirty fought with all their might, slithering against the queen's soapy body. Every time she tried to climb out of the bath, they jumped on her head and forced her back. Every time the guards advanced, Mendax's voice mewed bravely from inside the Power Hat, "Back – or I'll turn you all into slugs!" As long as his small head was in that hat, he was invincible. Not even the super-magic of the queen could harm him.

His mews were becoming fainter. The grip of his claws was loosening. Old Noshie and Skirty Marm splashed and biffed, and still Mrs Abercrombie brushed them off as if they were flies. But at last Skirty Marm got the Power Hat on her own head – with the sodden, exhausted Mendax still lying, half drowned, inside it.

The guards immediately bowed low. Mrs Abercrombie was a witch of brilliance – but whoever wore the Hat was the strongest witch in the world and rightful Queen of the Island. Her hideous face turned deathly pale.

Crossing her fingers, Skirty Marm muttered a spell.

A pinkish ooze surged out of the overflow in the bath. It spread across the water, and formed a sticky puddle around Mrs Abercrombie. There was a puff of smoke, and the ooze changed into Badsleeves and her Secret Liberation Army.

Mrs Abercrombie screeched and swore. She changed the army into slugs – but with the Hat on her head Skirty Marm could change them back with a single thought.

"You might as well give up!" said Badsleeves. "It'll soon be all over the island – the Reds have grabbed control of the Power Hat! If you want to be in charge again, you'll have to get yourself fairly and squarely elected! Now get out, and find yourself a cave. We're taking over your palace!"

Mrs Abercrombie, with a face of thunder, climbed out of the bath.

"Yuck!" cried Binbag, watching the soapy water sliding off her gigantic, wobbly body.

Badsleeves grinned. "Take her away. Don't worry if she tries any tricks – we've got the Hat."

"You'll pay for this!" rumbled Mrs

Abercrombie. "My Green and Purple subjects will stay loyal to me!"

Old Noshie had begun to eat the Royal Bath Snacks. "I wouldn't count on it!" she chuckled, with her mouth full of newts. Mrs Abercrombie's guards were meekly allowing the Liberation Army to push and prod them out of the crowded bathroom.

Mrs Abercrombie covered her unsavoury nakedness with an enormous grey towel. Distantly, they could all hear cheers, as news of her defeat spread across the island.

"Old Noshie and Skirty Marm," she growled, glaring at the witches, "I'll have my REVENGE on you two, if it's the last thing I do!"

Skirty Marm closed her eyes. Because the Power Hat was on her head, she saw green letters, rather like the letters on a computer screen. Options, said the letters. 1. Kill. 2. Squash. 3. Let her go, because you don't really care.

Number three, thought Skirty Marm. And Mrs Abercrombie, fuming and dripping, was led away by victorious Red-Stockings.

"Well done!" cried Badsleeves. "You can give me the Hat now."

"Not so fast!" said Skirty Marm.

"But Skirt, we did it!" protested Old Noshie. "Give her the wretched Power Hat so we can go home!"

"Sorry, Badsleeves," said Skirty Marm. "I'm keeping it. If I let you have it, how do I know you won't turn into another Mrs A.? How do I know you'll keep your promise and free the cat-slaves?" Gently, she picked up the exhausted Mendax. "We've done our bit. Now it's up to you to rule this island with true EQUALITY and JUSTICE."

Badsleeves scowled and stamped her foot. The other S.L.A.W. witches, however, looked pleased.

"She's got a point," said Binbag. "You must admit, Badsleeves, you were getting rather big for your stockings. I don't think we should trust any of our leaders with that Hat. It doesn't seem to bring out the best in a witch."

Badsleeves sighed. "Oh, I suppose you're right. But what will you do with it, Skirty? How do I know you won't try to be queen?"

"Pish and posh!" Skirty Marm said scornfully. "I've got better things to do. We'll take this Power Hat back to our new country and make

sure it never falls into the wrong hands again –
not even Mrs A. will be able to call it back. I'm
only going to use it for one small spell."

"What's that?" asked Old Noshie.

Skirty Marm grinned. "I'm collecting some
Lost Property."

She closed her eyes, and up flashed the magic
letters in her mind. Options: 1. Snatch bloomers
off Sneevil. 2. Snatch bloomers off Sneevil, and
smack her. 3. Snatch bloomers, and change
Sneevil into a little Yellow-Stocking.

"Number three again," said Skirty Marm.
"That'll teach her!"

8

A New Era

The first proper General Election on Witch Island was a magnificent event. Once the Purples and Greens realized Mrs Abercrombie no longer held the ultimate power, they were no longer terrified of her. This time, the Hat was not lost at sea, but firmly on the purple head of Skirty Marm. Noshie and Skirty were national heroines. They rode around on their broomsticks, shouting, "Vote Badsleeves!"

Mendax was having the time of his life. For once, he was allowed to make grand speeches to his heart's content. His finest moment had come when Old Noshie told him to free the kitchen cat-slaves. The poor creatures were afraid at first – but when they saw Mrs Abercrombie stomping out of the palace, they threw Mrs Wilkins in the sink and smashed all the crockery, and their happy purrs could be heard for miles.

Whether snooty or humble, the cats were now free citizens.

Skirty Marm kept the Power Hat on her head at all times so that it could not be tampered with. She had no idea what to do with it, but was determined to take it off the island. Several Purple-Stockings had offered her large sums of money if she would sell them the Hat. Mrs Abercrombie herself, now running her election campaign from a small and obscure cave, offered to share the Hat with Skirty. But Skirty Marm could not be bought.

"Think what you could do with it!" Badsleeves said rather wistfully. "Aren't you even tempted?"

"No," said Skirty Marm. "I've punished Sneevil, and that's my limit."

She was stern when Badsleeves suggested the Hat should be put in the Island Museum.

"Sooner or later, someone would smash the glass case and nick it," she said, looking hard at Badsleeves. "I'm going to think of a really safe place to hide it."

"We can ask Mr B.," said Old Noshie happily. Both witches were looking forward to telling their friend about their adventures. It was fun being national heroines, but Witch Island was no longer their real home. As Old Noshie put it, "Our hearts belong with the humans now."

They could not leave the island, however, until they had cast their votes at the election. Badsleeves won by a huge majority. As soon as she promised to lift the stocking freeze and put an end to the hated Broom Tax, she became hugely popular. Most Greens, and even Purples, were happy to vote for her. Though Mrs Abercrombie was still the cleverest individual witch, her power did not amount to much with thousands of Purples ranged against her.

"Let this day become a National Holiday," declared Chancellor Badsleeves, "in honour of the two brave witches who gave us LIBERTY!"

Old Noshie and Skirty Marm blushed with pride until their ears sizzled. They were invited to one hundred and sixty-four election night parties, and actually went to fifty-eight of them before Old Noshie fell asleep with her face in a bat tart.

"Dear me," said Mendax, "how very gratifying it is to be appreciated."

Chancellor Badsleeves had asked Mendax to be Minister of Cats in her new government. Old

Noshie and Skirty Marm were very surprised
when they heard he had refused this honour.

"I thought you'd love it," said Skirty Marm.
"You're such a show-off."

"Once, perhaps," purred Mendax. "But I
would miss my dear vicar far too much. And I
couldn't leave him to write his own sermons."

"I'm glad you're coming home with us," Old
Noshie said. "Know what, Mendax? If you
stayed here, I'd miss you!"

"Oddly enough," said Skirty Marm, "so
would I."

Mendax smoothed his whiskers. "I once

hated witches, but you two have showed me that you're not all like Mrs Wilkins." (Mrs Wilkins was in prison for cruelty to cats; Mendax had been chief witness at her trial.)

The following morning, Old Noshie, Skirty Marm and Mendax prepared to fly home. A large crowd gathered to see them off, and the Green-Stocking Brass Band played their latest hit, "March of the Main Sewer".

Chancellor Badsleeves awarded each of the three friends the Order of the Prune (First Class). Mendax tied on his saucepan crash-helmet, and climbed into his basket. The Power Hat was making Skirty Marm's head ache but, taking no chances, she rammed it down firmly across her forehead. The brooms set their course for home, and the witches looked over their shoulders at Witch Island until it vanished into a black speck in the black ocean.

They arrived home at tea time, and Mr Snelling and Mr Babbercorn were overjoyed to see them. Mr Snelling was so happy, he put his back out trying to turn a cartwheel. Mendax immediately put on his flowery apron and rushed to the kitchen to bake a homecoming sponge.

The vicar and the curate were amazed at the sight of the Power Hat. It certainly looked very strange and sinister standing in the middle of the sitting room carpet, tall as Mr Babbercorn. The everlasting candle burned with a still, ghostly light.

"I don't like keeping a . . . a thing like this on church property," said Mr Babbercorn, shaking his head. "What on earth shall we do with it?"

"It has to be somewhere near humans, but where humans can't get it," protested Skirty Marm. "Didn't we tell you how the pants you lent protected us? Mrs A. could never call it back from here – not with all her magic!"

Mr Babbercorn frowned. "Would the new extension to the village hall count? I mean, that's church property – and they've just dug the foundations."

"Perfect!" cried the witches.

As soon as it was quite dark, the curate and the witches carried the Power Hat through the streets of the village, and buried it deep in the foundations of the hall extension.

"It'll be covered in thirty metres of concrete tomorrow," said Mr Babbercorn breathlessly, tucking his spade under one arm.

"Good riddance!" said Skirty Marm. "I was getting so sick of wearing it. You can't even have a simple little thought in case it turns magic."

"Uneasy lies the head that wears the crown," Mr Babbercorn said solemnly.

They turned their backs on the Power Hat, and went back to the vicarage to eat Mendax's cake. The little cat made Mr Snelling very proud when he described his thrilling adventures without telling a single lie. Finally, yawning noisily, Old Noshie and Skirty Marm climbed the one hundred and eighty-six steps to their belfry.

It was bliss to lay their tired heads down on their Christmas cushions. The moonlight fell softly upon the great church bells. The woods and fields around them were cloaked in a velvet silence. All was peace.

Tired as they were, however, the witches could not fall asleep at once. The Power Hat had been buried, and would glow in secret under the village hall until the crack of doom. They could never forget it.

"Are you awake, Skirt?" asked Old Noshie.

"Yes," said Skirty Marm.

"I've been thinking," said Old Noshie, "that I've really had enough of magic."

"Me too," said Skirty Marm. "But I can't help wondering – has magic had enough of us?"

Red Stocking Rescue

For Dylan and Rowan

1

An Announcement

"You may now open the oven," Mendax said, "very gently so your cake doesn't sink. It's supposed to be a Victoria sponge – not a Victoria pancake!"

"Stop fussing!" growled Skirty Marm.

"Do as he says," urged Old Noshie. "You know we're rubbish at making cakes by ourselves!"

The vicarage kitchen at Tranters End was filled with a delicious smell of baking. It was also filled with a collection of characters you wouldn't normally expect to find in a vicarage.

Mendax was a small black cat. He was standing on his hind legs on the kitchen table. A flowered apron was tied round his waist, and his tail was tucked into the pocket to keep it out of the way. Old Noshie and Skirty Marm were two genuine witches, in black pointed hats and musty rags.

The witches had been pressing their noses against the oven door for the past half hour – and Mendax had been nagging them not to peep. The moment he gave his permission, the impatient pair opened the oven and carefully took out a round cake tin (they didn't need oven gloves, and they didn't burn their noses, because leathery witch-skin is not as delicate as the human sort).

"*Perfect!*" purred Mendax as the witches put the cake tin down on the cooling rack beside him. He tested the surface of the cake with his paw. "Nice golden colour, beautifully light, lovely smell – now, aren't you glad you followed my instructions?"

"Our first Victoria sponge," Skirty Marm said solemnly. It was such a great moment that she'd decided not to mind taking orders from a cat.

"Cor," murmured Old Noshie, "isn't it beautiful?"

The cake was for their best friend, Mr Babbercorn, who was coming home from his holiday that afternoon. He'd been away for two whole weeks.

Mendax sighed. "Poor Mr B., he works so hard. I do hope he's had a nice restful time."

"*We* certainly haven't," Skirty Marm said crossly. "And neither has the vicar. You've done nothing but boss, boss, boss, Mendax. I can't wait for Mr B. to come back and shut you up."

"Nonsense," said Mendax smugly. "He'll thank me for my splendid management."

Cuthbert Babbercorn was the curate at St Tranter's Church. A series of amazing adventures had brought the witches and Mendax to the sleepy English village of Tranters End. There had been some troublesome incidents at first, but the local people were now quite used to having witches in the church belfry and a rather bossy, talking cat at the vicarage.

These days, everyone in the village understood that although Old Noshie and Skirty Marm were ancient by human standards – over a hundred and fifty years old – they were very young for witches. The villagers had learned to make allowances for this unusual situation, and the witches had joined both the Brownies and the Old Folks' Drop-In Club. They often argued about which one they liked best. Skirty Marm liked singing with the Old Folks and hearing their interesting stories about human history. Old Noshie, less intellectual than her friend, preferred a brisk game of rounders with the Brownies.

Skirty Marm was tall and skinny, with a ragged mop of purple hair, a wrinkled grey face and gleaming red eyes. At witch school (as she was always reminding Old Noshie) she had been top of the class in everything. She had won the Spellbinder's Medal for thirty-six years in a row, plus two Golden Brooms for stunt flying, and the coveted Spitting Shield, not to mention various other prizes.

Old Noshie had never won anything except a Highly Commended badge for growing mould on a flannel. She was a short round witch, with bright green skin that glowed in the dark. Her wrinkled old head was as bald as an egg, and she usually wore a blue wig to keep it warm. She had great respect for Skirty Marm's wisdom and followed her in everything – which was not always a very good idea.

Both witches had picked up various human customs during their time in Tranters End, but there was one witchy thing they couldn't give up. Under their rags, each of them wore a pair of sagging, holey red stockings. They had been stripped of their official stockings when they left Witch Island, their old home, but their great friend Mrs Tucker, who ran the village post office and was also Brown Owl, had thrilled them by giving them new pairs.

I must explain that on Witch Island, where Skirty Marm and Old Noshie had grown up, you can tell a witch's age and importance by the colour of her stockings.

Yellow-Stockings are baby witches, studying basic magic at school. When they reach the age of one hundred, they become Red-Stockings and receive the Red-Stocking Spellbook. At the age of two hundred, they become Green-Stockings and are entitled to cast far stronger spells. Finally, at the age of three hundred, they become Purple-Stockings, the most powerful witches of all.

During Noshie and Skirty's time on Witch Island, the Purple-Stockings had been allowed to keep cat-slaves and to treat the younger witches like servants. The unfairness of it had driven the young Red-Stockings crazy. They hadn't dared disobey, however, because they lived in terror of the queen, Mrs Abercrombie.

This monstrous witch was nearly a thousand years old, hideously ugly and fiendishly clever.

Old Noshie and Skirty Marm would never have come to Tranters End in the first place if they hadn't sung a very rude song about Mrs Abercrombie at the Hallowe'en Ball. The furious old queen had banished them from the island. She might have forgotten about the song in a hundred years or so, but Old Noshie and Skirty Marm had since committed two far greater crimes. First, they had helped to lead a Red-Stocking revolution on the island, which had freed the cat-slaves and ended Mrs Abercrombie's cruel reign. Second – and far more serious – they had stolen the Power Hat.

The Power Hat was two metres tall, and an everlasting candle burned at its point. It was tremendously magical. No living witch knew how to awaken all its powers, but the witch who owned it became the strongest in the world. Without the Power Hat, Mrs Abercrombie was a fiendishly clever but ordinary Purple-Stocking, and only a few of her friends had voted for her when the first Witch Island elections were held after the Red-Stocking revolution. When last heard of, she was living in a small retirement-cave on the coast, casting spells to find the Power Hat and plotting her revenge.

Old Noshie and Skirty Marm hoped with all their hearts that the wicked ex-queen would never find the Power Hat. Mrs Abercrombie had recently written her memoirs (*My Stormy Passage*, Belch & Squelch, 10 witch shillings) and there was a whole chapter called "What I Will do to Old Noshie and Skirty Marm When I Get My Hat Back".

The two witches and Mr Babbercorn had hidden the Power Hat in the foundations of the new extension to the village hall at Tranters End. It had stayed there, perfectly peacefully, for over a year. Skirty Marm, however, was worried.

"I need to ask Mr B.'s advice about the you-know-what," she told Mendax and Old Noshie now. "I don't like what's happening at the village hall."

"Pish and posh," Old Noshie said gaily. "He'll be pleased with the changes."

While Mr Babbercorn was away on his holiday, there had been some peculiar goings-on. The hollyhocks outside the village hall had grown huge, with flowers the size of tubas. The terrible, tuneless church choir, which practised at the hall, had suddenly begun to sing like angels – only the week before, they had won first prize at a choir festival.

"I don't like it," Skirty Marm repeated, shaking her head. "It means the Hat's getting restless – and if it gives itself away, Mrs Abercrombie will find it."

"Oh, stop fretting," Old Noshie said. "Everything's fine – and we've just made a wonderful cake."

"A jolly good effort!" declared Mendax. His whiskers lifted in a smug smile. "Did I ever tell you about the sponge I baked under cannon fire at the Battle of Fungus Gulch?"

The witches groaned and rudely blew raspberries. In Latin, "Mendax" means *liar*, and the name suited this former cat-slave down to the tip of his glossy tail. He was absolutely addicted to telling tall stories.

Like all great liars, though, Mendax was very offended when people accused him of lying. "Not one of my best sponges, obviously," he said huffily. "I didn't have time to fold in the eggs. Would you like me to ice your cake?"

"Thanks, Mendax," said Old Noshie, "and could you write 'Welcome Home Mr B.' on it?"

"With pleasure. I know your spelling would never stand the strain."

"None of your cheek!" snapped Skirty Marm. Unlike the easy-going Old Noshie, she could never forget that Mendax had once been a spy, sent by Mrs Abercrombie to destroy them.

"Come on, Skirt," Old Noshie said quickly, "let's pick some nice weeds to decorate the tea table."

This had been Mr Babbercorn's first real holiday for years, and Old Noshie didn't want his homecoming to be spoiled by squabbling. Skirty allowed Noshie to drag her into the

garden. They gathered a fine bunch of dandelions, bindweed and thistles.

While the witches were arranging their weeds on the table, the vicar of St Tranter's Church, Mr Snelling, smelt cake and came out of his study. He was a smiling, roly-poly man, who was very fond of food.

"Oh, witches! What a spread!" he cried. "Victoria sponge cake, egg sandwiches *and* fairy cakes – and what's in these rolls?"

"Spiders," said Old Noshie, smacking her lips hungrily. "Fresh this morning. Do try one."

Mr Snelling made a face. "No thanks. I think I'll try a fairy cake."

"Leave those alone!" Mendax mewed sternly. "You don't get a bite to eat until you've finished writing your sermon!"

The vicar sighed. "You've got dreadfully above yourself, Mendax. I can't wait till Babbercorn comes home. He's the only person who can keep you in order!"

Mr Babbercorn had gone away a thin, pale, weedy young man. He returned with a healthy tan and fashionable new glasses.

"Cuthbert, you look simply wonderful," the

vicar said, with his mouth full of fairy cake. "Ah, there's nothing like the seaside. Gusty Bay must be a very refreshing place."

"It's a beautiful spot," said Mr Babbercorn. He heaved a deep sigh and smiled dreamily.

Mr Snelling was too busy eating to notice anything odd about Mr Babbercorn's behaviour, and the witches were too busy admiring the boxes of Gusty Bay fudge their friend had just given them.

"Eat up, Cuthbert!" cried Mr Snelling. "You haven't touched this excellent tea!"

Mr Babbercorn sighed again and helped himself to a spider roll. He would have taken a bite if Mendax hadn't snatched it out of his hand.

For the first time the vicar looked properly at Mr Babbercorn. "Cuthbert, what on earth is the matter with you? Ever since you arrived, we've had nothing from you but sighs and cheesy smiles."

Mr Babbercorn's face slowly blushed the colour of a radish. "I . . . I . . . I . . ." he stammered. "The fact is . . . I have an announcement."

He paused. The witches and Mendax waited

open-mouthed. Mr Snelling had frozen with a fairy cake halfway to his lips.

"The fact is," the young curate said in a rush, "I'M GETTING MARRIED."

There was a moment of stunned silence before the vicar threw the fairy cake into the air with a shriek of joy. "My dear Cuthbert, how romantic! Oh, what heavenly news!"

"HURRAH!" yelled Old Noshie and Skirty Marm. They were longing to see a human wedding – there was no such thing on Witch Island.

"Dear me," said Mendax, a faraway look in his bright green eyes. "Did I ever tell you about my little romance? It was spring in Paris, we were young and foolish – poor Fifi!"

The vicar giggled. "Do stop lying, Mendax. I want to hear all about the future Mrs Babbercorn!"

Back came the curate's dreamy smile. "Her name's Alice Wisk. I met her on the beach when she got her leg stuck in a deckchair. She works in a library and she's the prettiest, cleverest, kindest girl in the whole world!"

"Have you got a picture of her?" asked Old Noshie eagerly.

Mr Babbercorn had indeed got a picture of Alice. He took it carefully out of his pocket and showed it to his friends with bashful pride. The snap was of a sweet-faced young woman with curly brown hair and a lovely smile. She was sitting on a giant toadstool in a park, eating a "99" ice cream.

"Charming!" declared the vicar, with a sigh of delight. "Quite charming!"

Skirty Marm peered at the photograph and gasped, "She's as beautiful as a princess – I can't wait to see her in her white dress!"

"It's a shame you can't wear one too," Old Noshie told Mr Babbercorn. "You'd look great."

Mr Babbercorn laughed. "I'm afraid only the bride gets the white dress."

Mr Snelling cut himself a large slice of sponge cake. "Do you know," he said, "I've often wondered why you don't have weddings on Witch Island. I mean – where do little witches come from?"

"We're grown from seed," explained Skirty Marm. "We get our Yellow-Stockings as soon as we're ready to leave the potting sheds. It's not like humans at all."

"Not at all," agreed the vicar and the curate.

Old Noshie was still gazing at the photograph. "When can we meet Alice?"

"Oh," said Mr Babbercorn, "ah."

His face, which had been so red, turned white. "She's coming to Tranters End next week – but there's a slight problem."

"What problem?" asked the vicar.

Mr Babbercorn hung his head. "I haven't exactly told her about the magic."

Mr Snelling groaned. "Oh, Cuthbert!"

"Well, it'll be a nice surprise for her," said Old Noshie happily. "Perhaps we can do a few little spells to make her feel welcome."

"No!" squeaked Mr Babbercorn, horrified.

"You really should have mentioned something before you invited her here," said Mr Snelling.

"I know," sighed Mr Babbercorn, "but there was never a right moment. How on earth do you tell the woman of your dreams that you live with two witches and a talking cat?"

"I can see it might be tricky," Mr Snelling admitted.

"Anyone would think," said Mendax coldly, "that you were *ashamed* of us."

"Oh, please don't think that!" Mr Babbercorn cried. "You're all my dear friends, and I know Alice will love you as much as I do. But, can't you see – I have to warn her about you first!"

Old Noshie was frowning. "I suppose so," she said grudgingly. "She might be scared of witches."

Mr Babbercorn looked pleadingly at his three magical friends. "Just at the beginning," he said, in a hesitant and embarrassed voice, "just to start with, I'd be very grateful if you witches would stay out of sight – and if Mendax could behave like an ordinary cat."

"*Ordinary!*" Mendax shuddered.

"I'll tell her as soon as she's settled in, honestly!"

"All right," Old Noshie said crossly. "We'll stay out of sight – won't we, Skirt? Just at first."

Mr Babbercorn looked hard at Skirty Marm. "Do you promise?"

"Oh, I promise," Skirty Marm said distantly.

Only Old Noshie noticed that Skirty Marm had her fingers crossed.

2

Dear Old Souls

Mr Babbercorn was a popular young curate. The announcement that he was getting married filled the people of Tranters End with delight. Everyone was longing to meet Alice Wisk.

"Her first day here will be quite a social whirl," Mendax told the witches on the morning of Alice's visit. "Lunch with the churchwardens, tea at the Old Folks' Drop-In Club, a visit to the Brownies, and dinner with the bishop." He licked his paw gloomily. "And they won't even let me help with the food! I have to sit in the sun, rub myself against people's legs, play with stupid toys—"

He broke off, shuddering. "I simply *loathe* behaving like an ordinary cat. I'll completely lose the respect of the mice."

"We're Brownies *and* Old Folk!" sniffed Old Noshie. "It's MEAN not to invite us! I would have thought Alice would be pleased to meet two nice witches. She might ask us to be her bridesmaids!" Old Noshie longed to be a bridesmaid.

"And if she was allowed to hear my voice," said Mendax, "I'm sure she'd *beg* me to sing a solo at her wedding."

Skirty Marm was in a rage. She stormed around the church belfry where she and Old Noshie lived, raising a cloud of dust from the splintery wooden floorboards.

"It's just NOT FAIR!" she shouted. "It

would serve that mean, stinky, selfish curate right if we—"

The rest of her speech was drowned out by a tremendous "CLANG!" which made the whole belfry shake. The church clock was striking twelve, and the two enormous bells made a deafening racket. Mendax turned pale under his black fur and streaked away down the one hundred and eighty-six belfry steps. The witches, however, rather liked the noise.

When it was over, Old Noshie said, "Sorry, Skirt – I didn't quite catch that."

Skirty Marm's red eyes were dangerously thoughtful. "I've just had one of my ideas," she said.

"Have you?" Old Noshie tried not to sound dismayed. Skirty Marm's ideas usually led straight to trouble.

"Listen," said Skirty Marm. "Mr B. doesn't want Alice to meet witches. Right?"

"You know it is, Skirt – in case she changes her mind about marrying him."

"Suppose we're *not* witches?" Skirty Marm smiled craftily. "Suppose we're just ordinary members of the Old Folks' Club? We could join them for tea at the vicarage, and Mr B. wouldn't have any excuse to throw us out. Besides, it would make it easier to tell Alice about us when the right time comes!"

Skirty Marm was getting excited as the flame of her genius burned higher. "He'd only have to say something like, 'Alice, remember those two old ladies from the Drop-In Club? Well, they're witches.' *Simple!*"

Old Noshie's green face was doubtful. "It'd never work. Alice would notice our pointed hats straight away."

Skirty Marm gave her friend a quick biff on the head. This sometimes helped Old Noshie to organize her muddled thoughts.

"You silly old bag, that's the whole point! We wouldn't be wearing our hats! We'd be disguised as two REAL OLD LADIES!"

The boldness and brilliance of this plan took Old Noshie's breath away. "But how would we do it?" she gasped. "We haven't any human clothes."

"We'll sneak into the jumble room at the village hall," said Skirty Marm excitedly, "where they keep all the things that don't sell at jumble sales."

"But what about my green skin?"

Skirty Marm had forgotten about this, but thought quickly. "We'll borrow some face paint from the Drama Club," she said. "I'm sure I saw a stick of white in their cupboard. We could say you're pale with happiness. And I'll say my skin's gone grey because of too much joy!"

Old Noshie had caught on at last and she was beaming like a lighthouse. "We wouldn't even be breaking our promise to Mr B.," she said. "Because we only promised we wouldn't let Alice see two witches. She won't even notice two more old ladies!"

Skirty Marm peeped out of the big belfry window. She had to make sure the coast was clear, since the whole village had been sworn to secrecy about the local magic. To the witches' annoyance, everyone had agreed that coming face to face with it on her first visit might put poor Alice off marrying their curate. They all remembered how shocked they'd been at first themselves.

The village street was deserted. So was the vicarage. Mr Babbercorn and Mr Snelling had driven off in the vicar's car to meet Alice at the station. Mendax was sulking in the garden shed. Not a soul saw Old Noshie and Skirty Marm fluttering down from the church belfry to the village hall on their broomsticks.

The Power Hat was hidden underneath the new extension to the hall, but there was no time to worry about it now. Skirty Marm absent-mindedly checked the gigantic hollyhocks outside the hall and pulled out a dandelion that had grown to the size of a cabbage.

While Old Noshie ate the dandelion (she never could resist a juicy weed), Skirty Marm mumbled a quick spell to open the window of the jumble room. It was high up, and rather small, but Skirty Marm was a nimble witch and she scrambled up easily. Old Noshie, twice as plump and not nearly so nimble, had to be pulled up by her friend.

When they were both safely inside the small airless jumble room, the two witches gazed around in wonder. It was crammed from floor to ceiling with heaps of jumble – bags of clothes, boxes of dusty old books, battered bits of furniture.

"*Wow!*" cried Old Noshie. "Look at all this treasure!" She picked up a picture, in a broken frame, of some white horses running on a beach. "Why would anyone give a beautiful thing like this to a jumble sale? It would look very elegant in our belfry."

Skirty Marm had found a large shopping bag made of bright pink plastic. "Very tasteful," she remarked. "I'll use this to carry my witch-clothes. I'd hate my best rags to get sold at a jumble sale by mistake."

"We'll bring it all back," Old Noshie said, "so it won't be like stealing. Except the picture. Don't these horses look real? You can almost taste them!"

Skirty Marm wasn't listening. She had just found something amazing and extraordinary in the pink bag. "Nosh – look!"

Like a conjuror pulling a rabbit from a hat, she drew from the bag a large brown bottle of Nasty Medicine.

Now, as every human being ought to know, drinking someone else's Nasty Medicine is a very STUPID and DANGEROUS thing to do – practically as bad as taking POISON. Witches are not humans, however, and on Witch Island, Nasty Medicine is considered a great treat. All it does to witches is to make them disgracefully tipsy.

In the past, this revolting drink had got Old

Noshie and Skirty Marm into terrible trouble. You could say that it had been their downfall, since it was Nasty Medicine that had inspired them to sing the rude song about Mrs Abercrombie. You'd think they would have seen enough of it – they had sworn to Mr Babbercorn that they would never touch another drop – but both witches stared at the brown bottle with greedy longing.

"We can't just leave it in the bag, can we?" Old Noshie asked hopefully.

Skirty Marm was stern. "Certainly *not*! Putting it back in that bag would be terribly careless of us. What if some poor human drank it? No, Noshie. It is our DUTY to drink this Nasty Medicine AT ONCE, before it falls into the wrong hands."

"I quite agree!" cried Old Noshie.

Skirty took the top off the bottle. "I don't want to get you into trouble, Nosh – so I'll drink it."

"OH, NO YOU DON'T!" roared Old Noshie. "Gimme my share, you thieving old weasel, or I'll squash your nose!"

She slapped Skirty Marm. Skirty Marm slapped Old Noshie. An unseemly scuffle broke out, during which Old Noshie rammed Skirty Marm's head into an old suitcase, and Skirty Marm threw Old Noshie's blue wig out of the window.

Finally, they settled the argument by making a fingermark on the label of the bottle and drinking exactly half each. The Nasty Medicine was out of date (which made it even more dangerous to humans) and smelt so incredibly disgusting that no human would have touched it anyway.

"DEE-LICIOUS!" cried Skirty Marm.

"YUM-YUM!" cried Old Noshie.

And as drunken witches do, they began to sing a vulgar song.

"Medicine Molly is my name –
Medicine-guzzling is my game!
There's no other drink like ME-DI-CINE –
It makes you giggle and it makes you grin!

All round the island it's the same –
For ME-DI-CINE I got my name!
Excuse me while I lie down in the gutter –
Medicine Molly is my name!"

Then (as drunken witches do) they cried a little and swore eternal friendship. Neither was at all ashamed of her disgraceful and appalling behaviour.

Nasty Medicine always made Skirty Marm feel very brave and clever. "Now for our costumes!" she cried. "Do what I do, Nosh – remember, we have to talk like the other Old Folk at the Drop-In Club. It couldn't be easier."

Old Noshie hiccuped loudly. "Lucky Alice – now she's going to meet the most interesting old ladies in Tranters End!"

*

By tea time, Mr Babbercorn was feeling a little anxious. Alice had arrived safely at the vicarage, and the lunch with the churchwardens had been a splendid success. Mendax had kept well out of sight – except once, when he was seen chasing a bird across the lawn.

Alice had said, "What a sweet cat!"

All in all, everything was going beautifully. But Mr Babbercorn had expected to see the faces of the witches at the top of the church tower, peeping out of the belfry window – and there had been no sign of them.

"I don't like it," he whispered anxiously to the vicar. "They're up to something."

Mr Snelling was enjoying all the food and festivity. "Nonsense!" he said happily. "Noshie and Skirty are never naughty these days. You haven't seen them because they're being extra-good – I'm proud of them!"

"Hmmm," said Mr Babbercorn doubtfully. "I hope you're right."

The members of the Old Folks' Drop-In Club were walking up to the vicarage front door for their tea party. All the old ladies were wearing their best hats, and all the old gentlemen had flowers in their buttonholes. Mrs Miller, who played the piano at their sing-songs and liked to say she was "EIGHTY-THREE YEARS YOUNG", was carrying a large bunch of flowers for Alice.

Despite his worries about the witches, Mr Babbercorn felt very proud. Alice looks so pretty in her blue dress, he thought. She was passing around plates of cakes and shouting at deaf Miss Venables as if she'd lived in Tranters End all her life.

"That girl will be a blessing on the village," Mrs Miller told him. "I'm sure she'll soon get used to – to *you-know-who*."

Mrs Miller was a special friend of the witches who had introduced them to the Old Folks' Drop-In Club. She had invited them to tea in her cottage and told them to call her "Doris".

"Don't you fret, dear," she reassured the curate. "It couldn't be going better!"

At this moment, the doorbell rang again.

"That's funny," said Mr Snelling. "We're not expecting anyone else."

Mrs Miller went to answer the door. She came back into the sitting room a moment later with a very strange expression on her face.

"Something the matter, Doris?" asked Mr Snelling.

"N-n-no," Mrs Miller said doubtfully. "It's just that . . . er . . . two more members of our club have popped in unexpectedly."

"That's nice," said Alice, smiling.

Mr Babbercorn choked on a brandy snap. He knew exactly who these unexpected old folk would be, and it was too late to do anything about it.

To the horror of everyone except Alice, two very peculiar old ladies came shuffling into the room. One held a large pink shopping bag, stuffed with something dark. The other clutched a dusty picture.

"Well, dear. You must be Alice," said Skirty Marm in her best imitation of Mrs Miller. She shook Alice's hand. "Welcome to Tranters End, dear. My name is Miss Skirt, and this is my friend, Miss Nosh."

"Rubbish!" said Old Noshie loudly.

Skirty Marm hissed, "What are you talking about?"

Old Noshie hiccuped defiantly. "My name's not Miss Nosh – that's just stupid! I'm a dear old soul called Mrs Worksnap."

"How do you do," said Alice politely.

"I'm afraid Miss Nosh is a terrible old fool, dear," Skirty Marm said sternly. "Take no notice of her. I've no idea where she got this 'Worksnap' business."

Mr Babbercorn tugged at the vicar's sleeve. "This is *ghastly*!" he whispered frantically. "Heaven knows where they found it, but I'd swear those two have been at the Nasty Medicine – they stink of it! We've got to get rid of them!"

Alice was a very polite young woman, but she couldn't help staring. Both these strange old ladies wore knitted hats, pulled down low over their foreheads – Miss Skirt's hat seemed to be a tea cosy. The face of Miss Nosh (or "Mrs Worksnap") was covered in thick white paint. The backs of her ears appeared to be bright green. The face of Miss Skirt was an unhealthy shade of grey, and her eyes were hidden behind a pair of sunglasses. Although the weather was warm, both Miss Nosh and Miss Skirt were wrapped in thick brown coats and wore lumpy brown stockings.

"Do have a scone," said Alice, holding out a plate to the two witchy ladies.

"YUM!" shouted Old Noshie.

Skirty Marm nudged her, to remind her that they were supposed to be behaving like senior humans.

"I don't mind if I do, dear," Skirty Marm said, in her best Mrs Miller voice.

Alice glanced curiously around the room. Everyone – except Miss Nosh and Miss Skirt – had gone very quiet. Mr Babbercorn was as pale as his own white collar. Mr Snelling had begun to hum (as he always did when he was feeling nervous).

"Do sit down," Alice said kindly to the two old ladies.

"I'm afraid you'll have to SPEAK UP, dear," Skirty Marm said. She was starting to enjoy being a real old lady. "I left my hearing aid on the draining board."

This had once happened to a gentleman in the club called Mr Fisher, who now startled Alice by giving a sudden snort of laughter.

Skirty Marm plumped down on the sofa, pulling Old Noshie down beside her. There was a long uneasy silence.

Alice asked politely, "Have you lived here long?"

"AGES!" cried Skirty Marm.

"You must be full of wonderful stories about the village."

"COR, THAT'S PUTTING IT MILDLY!" shouted Miss Nosh.

Miss Skirt scowled and nudged her friend very hard.

"You'll have to excuse Miss Nosh, dear. She only sounds barmy because she's been drinking."

Mr Babbercorn let out a strangled yelp. Mr Snelling choked on a spoonful of trifle, spraying jelly far and wide. Mrs Miller and Mr Fisher were struggling not to giggle.

"We're a marvellous old pair," Skirty Marm went on. "Got all our marbles."

"Oh, I'm sure," said Alice.

"I always say, I'm A HUNDRED AND FIFTY-THREE YEARS YOUNG!"

"Goodness," said Alice. "What a tremendous age!"

"And I feel the cold," said Skirty Marm. "Even in summer, I never go out without two thick pairs of bloomers. Want to see them?"

Mr Babbercorn could bear no more. He leapt to the sofa and grabbed each witch by their bony hands.

"I'm afraid Miss Nosh and Miss Skirt have to leave now," he said firmly.

"No we don't," protested Old Noshie. "We haven't had any trifle."

"Yes, you do," said Mr Snelling, wiping jelly off his face with a tissue. "You have to leave *right now*."

Mr Babbercorn looked so angry that the dear old souls on the sofa sobered up at once. Even Miss Skirt realized, with a sinking heart, that the two most interesting old ladies in Tranters End were in very hot water indeed.

3

Dear Old Souls in Trouble

The telling-off took place in the belfry, early the next morning. Mr Babbercorn lectured Old Noshie and Skirty Marm for over an hour, but here is a brief summary of the points he covered.

1. He had never been so embarrassed in his life. Especially by:
   a) The ridiculous disguises worn by the witches.
   b) Skirty Marm's public mention of "bloomers" at a vicarage tea party.
   c) The obvious reek of Nasty Medicine.
2. Alice now thought she was coming to a village full of completely mad old ladies.
3. The witches had broken two major promises:
   a) That they would keep away from Alice, and
   b) that they would never touch another drop of Nasty Medicine.

4. Thanks to the awful behaviour of the witches, it would now be even more difficult for Mr Babbercorn to tell Alice about the magic at Tranters End.

Old Noshie and Skirty Marm listened in silence, looking very sulky and feeling terrible – they had both woken up with thumping headaches.

If Mr Babbercorn was looking for signs of remorse, however, he was disappointed. Neither witch was sorry. They were still furious with the curate for bundling them out of the vicarage tea party so rudely. Afterwards, they had flown up to the roof and shouted "BUM!" down the chimney.

"How could you do it?" cried Mr Babbercorn. "You knew how important it was for Alice to get a good impression!"

Skirty Marm scowled. "If you didn't like our disguises, you should have invited us to the party as *ourselves*. It's all your fault because you tried to hide us."

"YES!" shouted Old Noshie. She was not as clever with words as Skirty Marm, but she supported her friend by shouting "YES!" every few minutes.

"All you had to do was wait." Mr Babbercorn groaned. "I was going to introduce you to Alice at the right moment!"

His thin cheeks reddened as he said this. He knew it was the weakest part of his argument. Deep down, in his heart of hearts, he did rather wish that Alice didn't have to know about the witches. They thought he was ashamed of them, and he couldn't really deny it. Alice was the sweetest girl in the world, but what if she was shocked when she found out about the witches – and refused to marry him?

He sighed. "Witches, listen – I was cross yesterday, but Alice was very nice about it. Especially when I told her that Miss Nosh and Miss Skirt were leaving the village immediately."

"*Leaving?*" Skirty Marm was suspicious.

"Yes, and Alice is coming to stay in Tranters End." Mr Babbercorn hurried on, rather guiltily. "She's going to rent the spare room at Mrs Miller's cottage. Now, witches, I beg you – keep out of her way until I've explained about the magic!"

"Oh, *we'll* stay out of the way all right," said Skirty Marm with a dangerous glint in her eye.

("YES!" shouted Old Noshie.)

"Thank you," said Mr Babbercorn.

Skirty Marm smirked scornfully. "But I can't answer for Miss Nosh and Miss Skirt. Until you've explained to Alice, you're going to see a lot of those two!"

The poor young curate trudged down the one hundred and eighty-six belfry steps, feeling very worried and very sad. He knew he had deeply offended the witches by not introducing them to Alice straight away. And now they wanted to punish him. His spirits sank as he prepared himself for the difficult days ahead.

To Mr Babbercorn's dismay, Miss Nosh and Miss Skirt were waiting – wearing their ridiculous costumes – outside Mrs Miller's cottage on the day Alice moved in.

"Dear old souls," said Alice. "I thought you said they'd left."

"They've come back," Mr Babbercorn said gloomily.

"They seem very kind," Alice said, "but ever so odd. Miss Skirt can't really be a hundred and fifty-three! And why does Miss Nosh plaster herself in that white stuff?"

"It's ointment," lied the curate miserably.

"She suffers from a rare skin disease."

"Poor old thing," sighed Alice. "Well, I'll look forward to seeing a lot of them, now I'm here."

And see a lot of them she certainly did. For the next two weeks, every time Mr Babbercorn tried to be alone with the woman he loved, out would pop Miss Nosh and Miss Skirt. They haunted Alice like a pair of barmy old ghosts.

When Alice and Mr Babbercorn went for a romantic stroll beside the river, there were Miss Nosh and Miss Skirt – sitting on the bank with their tongues sticking out.

"Why are they doing that?" wondered Alice.

"They're catching flies," said Mr Babbercorn, wincing as Old Noshie gulped down a dragonfly. "Ignore them."

Alice giggled. "It's like that song about the old woman who swallowed a fly. I didn't think it happened in real life!"

The vicarage garden was full of roses and extremely pretty. When Mr Babbercorn tried sitting there with Alice, however, he quickly noticed two beady pairs of eyes, and two pointed noses sticking through the trellis.

"Shouldn't we invite them in?" asked Alice.

"No," Mr Babbercorn said loudly.

He was beginning to be very annoyed with Old Noshie and Skirty Marm. The more they haunted Alice, the more determined he was not to tell her a thing until they stopped behaving so rudely.

In church, during the hymn "Guide Me, O Thou Great Redeemer", the witches sang "Tell Her, O Thou Stinky Curate!"

Skirty Marm, in particular, was at least as determined as Mr Babbercorn.

The curate was a gentle and kind-hearted man, but his patience was being stretched to its limit. It snapped one warm evening when he took Alice for a walk in the woods.

Just as he was murmuring, "Isn't this peaceful?", there was a sound of snapping wood, and Old Noshie crashed down from a tree on to the path in front of them.

"Good gracious," said Alice. "Are you hurt, Miss Nosh?" Polite as she was, she couldn't help looking astonished. She had never met any very old ladies who climbed trees.

"I told her that branch was rotten," said Skirty Marm's voice from above them.

Old Noshie stood up, rubbing her bottom. "I wanted to get a good view!"

"Miss Skirt," said Mr Babbercorn sternly, "kindly come down from that tree."

"NO!" shouted Skirty Marm. "I WON'T!"

"Excuse me, Alice," Mr Babbercorn said, through gritted teeth. "Would you mind walking back to Mrs Miller's by yourself? I have some urgent business to settle, with Old . . . I mean, with Miss Nosh and Miss Skirt."

"Of course I don't mind," said Alice, secretly wondering why her future husband looked so cross. "Good evening, ladies."

As soon as she'd gone, the curate snapped, "Skirty Marm – DOWN!"

And his voice was so strict that Skirty Marm scrambled down from her tree at once.

"This," said Mr Babbercorn, "has got to stop!"

Skirty Marm stuck out her lip stubbornly. "It'll stop when you tell Alice we're really witches."

"I'm not saying a word to her," said Mr Babbercorn, "until I've gone at least two weeks without seeing Miss Nosh and Miss Skirt."

"Two weeks!" wailed Old Noshie. "We can't hide for two whole weeks!"

"Alice will wonder what's happened to the

dear old ladies," Skirty Marm pointed out smugly.

"I'll say they've both been killed in a freak accident!" shouted Mr Babbercorn, losing his temper at last. "Because if this persecution goes on for much longer it won't be far from the truth! I've a good mind to stuff the pair of you into a wheelie bin and pay the dustmen to take you away! Witches, you have got to leave us alone!"

With this, Mr Babbercorn stomped angrily away through the woods – the mild young curate, who had never stomped in his life.

There was a moment of silence while the witches stared after him, their mouths gaping with surprise.

Old Noshie burst into tears. "Oh, Skirt! What have we done? We were MEAN to our friend – and now he doesn't want to see us EVER AGAIN!"

"Huh! I don't care!" said Skirty Marm.

But she didn't sound very sure. For the truth was, she *did* care – very much indeed. Life without Mr Babbercorn would be as dull and flavourless as bat pudding without treacle.

4

Emergency

Old Noshie was still crying when the witches went to bed that night. Her tears had washed away her "Miss Nosh" face paint, so that her woebegone cheeks were striped green and white.

Skirty Marm was still putting up a great show of not caring, but finding it harder and harder to hide her misery. This was the worst quarrel they'd ever had with their best friend.

The misery of the witches didn't last long, however. In the middle of the night, when the moon rode high above St Tranter's Church, the witches were woken by a loud hammering on the belfry door.

It was Mr Babbercorn, and he looked dreadful – pale as a ghost, with all his hair standing on end. He was gasping for breath because he had just pelted like lightning up the one hundred and eighty-six steps.

"Witches, you've got to forgive me – I need your help!"

Old Noshie and Skirty Marm understood at once that Something Terrible had happened. Skirty Marm fetched the curate her cushion (there were no chairs in the belfry), and Old Noshie put the kettle on (which is always a good thing to do in an emergency).

When he'd got his breath back, Mr Babbercorn gasped, "It's Alice – she's VANISHED!"

Old Noshie cried, "Oh, no! She's run away because we were naughty!" And she was all set to burst into tears again.

"Shut up, fusspot," said Skirty Marm, not unkindly. "Alice wouldn't just run away, would she, Mr B.?"

"*Never!*" Mr Babbercorn said firmly. "Alice would never go anywhere without telling me. But witches, I can't ask you for help until I've apologized. I admit that I wasn't as proud as I should have been to have the two of you as my friends. I should have introduced you to Alice straight away. I'm not asking you to help for my sake, but if you care at all about Alice—"

He broke off, and a tear rolled down his pale cheek.

Old Noshie and Skirty Marm were deeply touched by this noble apology.

"We're sorry too," said Skirty Marm. "We know it was very cheeky to spy on you – don't we, Nosh?"

"We'll *never* do it again!" Old Noshie wiped her nose on her sleeve, leaving a smear of white face paint.

Mr Babbercorn wiped his nose on a proper handkerchief. "Dear witches, it's all forgotten now. Alice has vanished, and you are the only people in the world I can turn to!"

Old Noshie made them all a refreshing cup of warm rainwater with a spoonful of mud (witches hate human tea), and Mr Babbercorn told them the story of Alice's mysterious disappearance.

Nobody had seen her since she left the witches and Mr Babbercorn in the woods. She hadn't returned to Mrs Miller's cottage, and Mrs Miller had telephoned the vicarage two hours ago, very worried.

"The vicar and Mendax and I searched the woods for her, calling her name, but there was no sign of her." Mr Babbercorn sipped his rainwater without seeming to taste it, which was probably just as well. "We got home, and I was just about to ring PC Bloater when something fell down the chimney."

Turning a shade paler, Mr Babbercorn took the "something" out of his jacket pocket and gave it to Skirty Marm. It was a thick piece of paper, smeared with soot and dirt. On it was scrawled in blotted brown ink:

"IF YOU WANT ALICE GIVE ME
THE HAT!"

"AAARGH!" screamed Old Noshie, dropping her cup. "It's the queen! The queen's stolen Alice!"

"Pull yourself together!" ordered Skirty Marm. "This is no time to panic!"

"YES IT IS!" Old Noshie wailed.

Skirty Marm turned to Mr Babbercorn. "This note is definitely from Mrs Abercrombie, Queen of the Witches."

Mr Babbercorn nodded sadly. "That's what Mendax said. He said it was no use calling PC Bloater. He said Mrs Abercrombie would *stop at nothing* to get her hands on that Power Hat."

"But how did Mrs A. do it?" cried Old Noshie. "She doesn't have the power to go around kidnapping humans!"

Skirty Marm was gloomy. "Don't you remember anything from school, you daft old brush? A witch can always kidnap a human if she wants to. Alice must have left a loophole."

"A loophole?" Mr Babbercorn was bewildered.

"It's when a human does something that allows magic in," Skirty Marm explained. "Maybe Alice trod on hemlock with her left foot, or walked round the church with her back to the sun, or forgot to kiss the first hare she saw by moonlight. Those things don't normally matter – unless a witch is watching you like a hawk, *waiting to pounce*."

Mr Babbercorn had never seen the ex-queen of the Witches, but he had heard enough about her to make him shudder now. The thought of the horrible old monster waiting to pounce on his Alice was awful.

"Where do you think Mrs Abercrombie has taken her?" he whispered desperately. "Can you bring her back?"

"We *have* to," said Skirty Marm, getting gloomier by the minute. "If we can't find Alice by ourselves, we'll have to give Mrs A. the Power Hat. And if we give her the Hat—"

"She'll KILL us!" Old Noshie finished for her.

"I won't allow you to give up the Hat," Mr Babbercorn said bravely. "I know Alice would say the same. But – can anything be done?" His eyes were pleading, and so were Old Noshie's.

Skirty Marm was thinking so hard her purple hair crackled with electricity. She'd won the Spellbinder's Medal for thirty-six years in a row, but could she handle something as tough as this? Did she dare to fight a battle of wits with Mrs Abercrombie?

"There's the advanced finding spell," she said slowly. "I've only done it once. It's ever so tricky."

"I remember!" Old Noshie began to dance with excitement. "You used it to find my singing yo-yo when I dropped it in the sea! Don't worry, Mr B. – our chemistry teacher said Skirty was the best finder in the school!"

Skirty Marm was not at all sure she could remember the whole of this complicated spell, but she hated to disappoint the poor curate.

"We'll give it a try," she declared, doing her best to sound very confident. "Nosh, nip outside

299

and catch me an old pigeon – one with plenty of mites."

"Righty-ho!" shouted Old Noshie. She grabbed her broomstick and jumped out of the belfry window – a sight that always made Mr Babbercorn dizzy. He watched as Skirty Marm picked up her pointed hat and started to fill it with various strange ingredients.

"Let me see . . . dried slugs, powdered frogspawn – drat, we're nearly out of beetle's elbows—"

Old Noshie crashed back into the belfry, clutching an ancient smelly pigeon. "Have we got everything, Skirt?"

"We need some salt, some bicarbonate of soda and a bar of soap." Skirty Marm was frowning with the effort of recalling the spell. "We'd better go down to the vicarage."

Mr Babbercorn jumped up eagerly, glad to be doing something. Old Noshie stuffed the cross old pigeon into her hat, jammed it on her head and picked up the iron cauldron they had got mail-order from Witch Island. It was very heavy, but witches are stronger than humans and she carried it as easily as a sack of feathers. The three of them ran down the one hundred and eighty-six belfry steps and out into the warm summer night.

The houses along the village street were dark, but the windows of the vicarage blazed with light. In the kitchen they found Mendax, and the vicar in his dressing gown. Mr Snelling sprang out of his chair the moment he saw the witches.

"Thank heavens! You've got to find poor Alice!"

His eyes grew round with amazement as Skirty Marm unpacked her hatful of ingredients onto the kitchen table.

Mendax stood on his hind legs and tied on his apron. "Let me help. I've assisted at a finding spell before – and I'm not lying," he added quickly. "I never lie in an emergency. It was when Mrs Wilkins lost her keys in the Main Sewer." (Mrs Wilkins was the nasty drunken old Purple-Stocking who had once owned the little black cat on Witch Island.) "I'll mash the dried slugs in milk," offered Mendax, "if someone else will drop in the pigeon mites."

"Drat, I forgot about that bird," said Old Noshie. "The mites'll be crawling all over my wig by now!" She took the pigeon out of her hat.

"YEUCH!" exclaimed the vicar. "What a revolting bird – it's got things living in its feathers!"

Mendax lit a candle and poured milk into his small, cat-sized saucepan.

"Mr Snelling," he mewed, "get your tweezers. Pick out the mites and drop them in while I stir."

"Oh, yes – anything!" Mr Snelling dashed to the bathroom for his tweezers, tripping over the cord of his dressing gown in his excitement.

"Mr B.," Skirty Marm said, "go into the garden and fetch me six blades of grass, a fresh caterpillar and a dandelion root."

Mr Babbercorn snatched up his torch and rushed out into the dark garden. Mendax stirred his saucepan above the candle flame. Old Noshie lit the gas under the cauldron. Soon, the vicarage kitchen had been transformed into a sorcerer's cave. The vicar and the curate, who did not normally approve of magic, followed Skirty Marm's instructions like a pair of sorcerer's apprentices.

Mr Snelling picked mites off the revolting old pigeon with his tweezers and dropped them one by one into Mendax's saucepan. Mr Babbercorn (sniffing to himself, because he was so worried about Alice) peeled and grated the dandelion root. Old Noshie and Skirty Marm muttered spells and stirred the bubbling cauldron – which looked very strange indeed, sitting on the vicarage stove.

"Pooh! What a pong!" complained Mr Snelling. "Do all spells smell as nasty as this?"

"Nasty?" Old Noshie was surprised. She thought the smell was delicious.

The kitchen was filling with dark blue smoke. Mendax added his saucepan of brownish gloop to the cauldron. As the little black cat moved, the pigeon shrieked and fluttered away out of the open back door.

"Huh! As if I'd eat an old fleabag like him," Mendax muttered scornfully. "I may be a cat, but I'm not *that* desperate."

Finally, the mixture was ready.

Skirty Marm bent over the cauldron and murmured the finding spell, praying she had remembered it correctly.

"Don't worry," Old Noshie whispered kindly to Mr Babbercorn. "We made it extra strong."

A loud rumble, rather like a huge burp, shook the cauldron.

"Here it comes!" shouted Skirty Marm.

Suddenly, to the astonishment of the vicar and the curate, the kitchen was jammed with things that had been lost. There were hundreds of coins from between the sofa cushions of every house in the village (when the vicar counted the money later it came to £246.83, which he gave to Oxfam). There were sixteen umbrellas, thirty-eight odd socks, two pairs of false teeth and Mr Fisher's pension book. Everything in Tranters End that had been lost was now found.

Except Alice.

There was a long silence.

Mr Babbercorn collapsed into a chair. "It didn't work!" he groaned.

"Excuse me," Skirty Marm was offended. "It worked perfectly!"

"Of course, of course," Mr Snelling said kindly. "Poor Cuthbert is simply worried about poor dear Alice. What on earth do we do now?"

"Nothing," said Old Noshie in a trembling voice. "If the advanced finding spell can't find her, it means she can't be found."

Yet again, she began to cry. It was terrible to think of Alice in the clutches of Mrs Abercrombie. Skirty Marm's lips wobbled. The vicar and the curate blew their noses. Mendax wiped his green eyes on his tail.

"Thanks, witches," Mr Babbercorn said quietly. "You did your best."

"Well, it's been nice knowing you all," gulped Old Noshie. "Me and Skirt will be dead quite soon, because we've got to tell Mrs A. where we hid the Power Hat, or we'll never see Alice again."

"*No!*" cried Mr Babbercorn. "I can't let you do it! There must be something else we can try!"

"Wait a minute!" Skirty Marm gave such a leap of excitement that her head banged against the ceiling. "What an *idiot* I am! Why didn't I think of it before? Never mind how strong Mrs A.'s spell is – our magic is even stronger, because WE'VE GOT THE HAT!"

She looked round at their gaping puzzled faces and stamped her foot impatiently. "Don't you see? The Power Hat can find anything in the whole world!"

"But . . . but . . . but . . ." stammered Old Noshie, "we buried the Hat!"

"Then we have to UN-bury it!" yelled Skirty Marm. "Come on!"

There was not a second to lose. Mr Snelling (still in his dressing gown and slippers) fetched four spades – and a small trowel for Mendax – from the garden shed. Quietly and fearfully, not knowing who might be watching, they crept through the dark village to the hall.

"Crikey," whispered the vicar, "look at the size of those hollyhocks! Why on earth couldn't old Mrs Whatsit spot where you'd buried the Hat?"

"Because without the Hat on her head she doesn't have enough power," said Skirty Marm. "Her tracking system just isn't sophisticated enough. Noshie, Mendax and I are protected by magical force fields which she can't penetrate at long-range," she explained. "So she must have operated some kind of advanced retrieval spell to kidnap Alice. Even without the Hat, Mrs Abercrombie is a very clever witch."

"But how can *we* get at the Power Hat?" Mr Babbercorn cried despairingly. "It's right under the foundations of the new extension!"

The witches and Mendax exchanged uneasy glances.

Mendax said, "Now, Vicar – I hope you're not going to be difficult about this—"

Before the words were out of his mouth, there was a blinding flash of light. The vicar and the curate were blown right off their feet into the shrubbery. Lumps of earth, brick and cement rained down on their heads.

When Mr Babbercorn had wiped the dust off his glasses, he gasped with horror. One side of the village hall lay in ruins. All that was left of the new extension was a heap of smoking rubble.

"Sorry about that," said Skirty Marm.

"My lovely extension!" moaned Mr Snelling. "Have you any idea how many jumble sales it took to raise the money for that?"

Mendax daintily spat out crumbs of plaster. "Do stop fussing, Vicar. Alice is worth a thousand extensions."

Skirty Marm looked into the large crater made by her magical explosion. The everlasting candle at the point of the Power Hat was poking out of the heap of debris, bathing everything in its eerie silver light. All the friends climbed down into the hole and quickly dug out the rest of the Hat.

"I don't know how I'm going to explain this to the churchwardens," puffed Mr Snelling, digging furiously. "And where are the choir supposed to practise now?"

The Power Hat had been buried under several metres of concrete. When the witches carefully brushed off the last bits of rubble, however, it was black, gleaming and perfect, without so much as a smudge or a dent. They pulled it out of the hole and placed it solemnly on the ground. It was taller than any of them.

Old Noshie shivered. "I don't like it. I've never liked that Hat."

Mendax said nothing, but jumped nervously into the vicar's dressing-gown pocket.

"Here goes," said Skirty Marm. She handed her own black pointed hat to Old Noshie and put on the Power Hat. She'd worn it before, while bringing it back from Witch Island, so she was prepared for the strange, buzzing, crowded feeling it gave the wearer's brain.

She closed her eyes and whispered, "Find Alice Wisk."

As she felt the might of the Power Hat surrounding her, Skirty Marm realized that Mrs Abercrombie had hidden Alice behind many layers of strong magic. She heard the Hat slicing through them, one by one. Then, inside her head, she saw green letters appearing – rather like the letters on an old-fashioned computer screen.

"*Alice is in the woods,*" she read aloud, "*at the north end of the bridge.*"

"But we've already looked for her there!" cried Mr Babbercorn. "I called and called her name!"

"The Power Hat is never wrong," said Mendax, popping his head out of the vicar's pocket. "Get a move on, Mr Snelling. We haven't a second to lose!"

The woods were pitch-dark. Mr Snelling and Mr Babbercorn switched on their torches, and the witches lit the ends of their fingers (this is not painful for witches). But they were all disappointed to reach the north end of the small wooden bridge and find no Alice.

Skirty Marm closed her eyes again. "You stupid old Hat – where's Alice?"

And again, the green letters appeared inside her head. "*None of your cheek!*" she read. "*Why don't you look properly? Third dock leaf from the big stone.*"

Skirty Marm didn't have time to be annoyed by the Hat's lofty tone. Torches and lighted fingers were instantly trained on the tangle of weeds beside the river.

"Well, I can't see a sausage," Old Noshie said crossly. "There's nothing here but a lot of *snails*."

The snails were oozing about under a row of dock leaves, groping blindly with their tiny horns.

"Just a minute," muttered Mendax. He jumped out of the vicar's pocket and disappeared among the weeds. A moment later, the others heard a long loud "Miaow!" of amazement and knew things must be serious – usually, the elegant cat thought miaowing rather vulgar. He came out of the weeds on his hind legs, carrying something very carefully between his front paws. It was a snail with a brown shell, a little larger than the others.

In the night silence of the woods, there was a very very quiet squeak, which sounded very much like "*Help*".

Mr Babbercorn shone his torch directly at the snail. If you squinted very closely, you could see a tiny face just under its horns. And that face had a definite look of . . .

"ALICE!" choked Mr Babbercorn.

5

The Professor

Naturally, Skirty Marm shut her eyes at once.

"Power Hat!" she shouted joyfully. "Let this snail be changed back into Alice Wisk!"

She waited for the green letters to appear inside her head. The waiting stretched into minutes. Skirty Marm saw nothing, except darkness.

"Come on!" she growled.

At last, the letters appeared. "*Search completed*," Skirty Marm read aloud. "*The metamorphic reach is outside my circle.*"

"Blimey," muttered Old Noshie. "What's that in Hinglish?"

Mr Babbercorn had turned so pale that his lips were grey.

"I think . . ." he choked. "I think the Hat is saying it can't help Alice."

The mouths of the witches dropped open in

312

amazement.

"But it *must* help her!" cried Mr Snelling. "You said it could do anything!"

Skirty Marm shut her eyes again. "Now look here, Hat – what's going on?"

The Hat typed, and she read, "*The human male in the collar is correct. The spell has been locked – by a locking charm from behind the Hills of Time. This is beyond my power. I can do nothing.*"

"NOTHING!" shouted Old Noshie. "Call yourself a Power Hat? We've been cheated!"

"What on earth are we going to do?" the vicar wondered miserably. "You can't have a wedding when the bride's a snail!"

"We won't give up," said Mr Babbercorn. "Be brave, Alice – we'll think of something!" And he took his snail-bride from Mendax and gently kissed her shell.

"It all happened in a flash," Alice squeaked in her tiny snail's voice. "One minute I was walking through the woods on two legs. The next minute I was sliding along on my stomach, leaving a disgusting trail of slime."

"Oh, please don't worry about your slime

trail," the vicar said kindly. "I think it's rather pretty."

"This has all been such a surprise," said Alice. "First being turned into a snail – and then finding the vicarage full of witches and talking cats. I keep thinking I must be dreaming!"

Mr Snelling sighed. "I wish you were!"

The snail that was Alice lay in a saucer on top of the kitchen table. Her friends sat around her, drinking cups of hot chocolate made by Mendax. They had explained the whole situation to the bewildered mollusc and were now trying to look cheerful.

"You're not to worry about anything," Mr

Babbercorn told Alice. "You can sleep quite comfortably in the old fish tank, and you must tell me which leaves you like best."

"Sorry I eat such an awful lot," squeaked the tiny voice. "I can't seem to help it. Those mulberry leaves were very tasty."

"I picked those," Old Noshie said proudly. "Is there anything else you fancy?"

"Well," Alice said, "now that you mention it, I can't stop thinking about thick cardboard."

"Ah, the brown sort," said Skirty Marm knowingly. "Yes, it is rather delicious."

While Alice was looking at Skirty Marm, Mr Babbercorn quickly wiped away two tears. He was doing his best to be cheerful for Alice's sake, but he felt that his dreams were in ruins. The poor young man was now imagining the writing on his tombstone:

"Cuthbert Babbercorn, Late Curate of this
 Parish,
Died of Grief when his Beloved was
 Transformed.
Also Alice, Snail of the Above."

The vicar's kind heart ached for his curate. "I wish I understood all that rigmarole about the

Hills of Time," he sighed. "What have they got to do with the Power Hat not being able to change Alice back?"

"We did it at school," Skirty Marm said. "The Hills of Time are where time began. The locking charm must have come from the Gardens Before Time."

"It all sounds very complicated," said Mr Snelling crossly.

Mendax put a pawful of mulberry leaves in front of Alice.

"Goodness knows how Mrs Abercrombie got her hands on such a valuable antique spell," he remarked. "She must have paid a fortune for it on the black market."

"You've lost me," complained the vicar. "Is there such a thing as an antique spell – like an antique chair or an old painting?"

"The Witch Island Museum is full of them," Mendax said. "Beautiful old spells, with gorgeous decorations." A faraway look came into his green eyes. "When I was a kitten, I often drew inspiration from those priceless works of art. As a matter of fact, I saw a very famous locking charm once – the Stumpenberg Trivet, as it is popularly known."

Old Noshie rudely blew a raspberry. "You LIAR! You've never seen the Stumpenberg Trivet! It's kept hidden away in case someone nicks it!"

Mendax was offended. "I didn't say I'd seen it in real life. I had a picture of it, on a calendar."

Skirty Marm scowled. "I bet Mrs Abercrombie used something like it, though. She wanted to make sure we could never reverse the spell unless we gave her that wretched Hat! Oh, I wish I'd never taken it!"

Mr Babbercorn's white face was thoughtful. "When we humans have something very old and precious, lots of scholars write about it. We put everything they write in libraries. Is there a library on Witch Island?"

Skirty Marm leapt to her feet. "Of course! The State Library! Nosh – we have to get in touch with Professor Mouldypage!"

"Don't be silly!" cried Old Noshie. "You wouldn't *dare*! And anyway, how would you find her? It's like a human trying to telephone the prime minister – impossible!"

Professor Mouldypage was in charge of the Witch Island State Library. She was an ancient, mysterious witch – older than Mrs Abercrombie

– and such a brilliant scholar that even the ex-queen treated her with respect.

Mendax smoothed his ears smugly. "You forget, I am a *radio expert*. During the Battle of Fungus Gulch, when the enemy had us cornered, I was the only one who could get the message through to headquarters—"

"Mendax, please stop lying," interrupted Mr Snelling. "We all know perfectly well that you were nowhere near the Battle of Fungus Gulch. You weren't even born then."

"Well, perhaps I wasn't the *only* one who radioed HQ," Mendax said, in an icy mew. "I exaggerate sometimes, as old soldiers will. Let us proceed to the shed."

In his days as one of the queen's spies, Mendax had contacted Witch Island on a secret radio set, hidden inside the garden shed. He still used it, to listen to the witch football and chat to his cat friends.

Now he led everyone through the dark vicarage garden. Mr Snelling carried a large torch, and Mr Babbercorn held Alice, on her saucer.

"Please don't lose hope," he whispered to her. "We'll move mountains to free you if we have to! And I'll always love you, Alice – even if you stay a snail!"

The four of them, plus Alice and Mendax, were rather a tight fit in the shed. Mr Snelling took out the lawnmower so they could all crowd round the radio.

Mendax put on his cat-sized headphones. His neat paws pressed buttons and turned dials. "I'm afraid I'm going to have to tell a few small lies," he said, "or we'll never get through."

After a great many stupendous lies, he

managed to get through to the cave of Professor Mouldypage.

Her musty dusty voice came crackling out of the radio. "What is the meaning of this impertinence? Who *dares* to disturb me?"

Both gabbling nervously at the same time, the witches poured out the sad story of Alice, Mr Babbercorn and the kidnapping.

"So, you want to unlock the spell," croaked the professor. "Why should I help you? Keep the Power Hat and let the human woman remain a snail."

Both witches gasped with horror.

"We don't care about the Hat!" shouted Old Noshie. "Alice is MORE IMPORTANT!"

Over the radio came a loud snort of anger.

"A little human being, MORE IMPORTANT than the mighty Power Hat? MORE IMPORTANT than the greatest symbol of our nationhood? I don't know what you young witches are coming to! In my day, you'd have *eaten* that curate of yours by now!"

Mr Babbercorn and Mr Snelling shuddered. To them, the rasping old voice sounded like all the wicked witches they had read about in fairy tales.

"In the land of the humans," Skirty Marm said, "people you love are more important than anything. If we can't turn that snail back into Alice, we'll have to give the Power Hat back to Mrs Abercrombie."

"And be killed in a horrible sort of way," Old Noshie couldn't help adding, "to be fixed on the morning of the execution, indoors if wet."

The professor's distant voice was full of amazement. "You care about the humans that much? You'd actually *die* for them?"

"Yes!" squeaked the witches, shaking in their ragged shoes.

"Well, burn my beard!" said Professor Mouldypage. To the witches' surprise, she chuckled. "I never liked Euphemia Abercrombie. Vulgar upstart – she was just the same at school. If you frcc your human without giving her the Hat, it'll serve THE OLD BAG RIGHT!" And she laughed her rusty laugh, like fingernails scratching a blackboard. "Heh, heh, heh!"

"Does that mean you'll help us?" gasped Mr Babbercorn.

"Yes, human," said the professor. "I do know a way. Don't imagine it will be easy. It might cost more than you are prepared to spend! To unlock the charm and reverse the spell, you need two berries from the Eert – that's the Backwards tree. It grows in the Gardens Before Time."

Skirty Marm groaned. She'd been hoping for a spell she could start right away. "But we don't know how to find the gardens!"

"Patience, young witch!" snapped the professor. "There is an entrance to the Gardens Before Time in the human world. If you find it and get through it, you'll earn your berries. Mrs Abercrombie has set you a trap, so don't take the Power Hat with you. Hide it somewhere safe."

"Our hiding place got blown up," Old Noshie said sadly.

"Into smithereens," added the Vicar.

"Then you must find a new one. And when you get the berries," the professor went on, "*if* you get them, perform a level six transforming spell backwards – leaving out the warts, and putting in the whole berries at the soft-boiled stage. Now, have you a pencil and paper? Put them down beside the radio."

Mr Snelling had a pencil in his pocket, and Old Noshie found a dusty paper bag. They watched as the pencil twitched, all by itself. Very quickly and neatly, it sketched out a map and marked one spot with an "X". The witches stared at it with round eyes – they were being shown one of the great secrets of the universe, beyond the reach of the Power Hat itself.

"Thanks, professor!" they chorused.

"This is very decent of you, Professor Mouldypage," said Mr Babbercorn. "Alice and I can't be grateful enough!"

"Oh, run along, run along!" shouted the professor, although she sounded quite pleased. "None of your *human mush*!"

The line went dead.

In the bright light of the vicarage kitchen, everyone stared at the map. It seemed to be a mass of straight lines and puzzling, squiggly writing.

"Londinium," read Old Noshie. "Where's that?"

"It's what the Romans used to call London," said Mr Snelling. "How fascinating! It must be a while since the professor visited the city."

"What's Pickydillo?" asked Mr Babbercorn anxiously. "And why has she written Cupid?"

323

The vicar smiled. "Another name for Cupid is Eros – it's the statue in the middle of Piccadilly Circus. So this long road must be Piccadilly."

He followed the road with his finger, and stopped at the cross. "Oh dear, this is rather inconvenient. It looks as if the entrance to the Gardens Before Time is right underneath my favourite shop!"

"Then that's where we'll go," declared Skirty Marm. "Give me the address."

"Oh, you can't miss it," said Mr Snelling smiling. "It's Fortnum and Mason's – one of the grandest and most famous food shops in the world!"

He coughed shyly. "I wonder, while you're there – could you pick up half a pound of chocolate almonds for me?"

6

A Visitor

There was no time to be lost. The witches began preparing for their journey to London the next morning. Mrs Miller – once she had got over the shock of Alice being a snail – was very helpful. To Mr Babbercorn's relief, she made some tactful suggestions about the outfits of "Miss Nosh" and "Miss Skirt". Old Noshie's face paint was changed from white to flesh colour, and Mrs Miller lent her a realistic brown wig to replace her blue one and cover her startlingly green bald head.

"I've nothing against green skin, dear," she said kindly, "but you have to look as much like proper humans as possible."

She lent Skirty Marm a real ladies' handbag made of shiny blue leather, and a more fashionable pair of sunglasses to hide her glittering red eyes. Both witches felt very elegant and stared at themselves in the mirror for ages.

"My hair looks like Alice's now," said Old Noshie. "I mean, like it did before she turned into a snail."

"Oh, *please* look after her!" begged Mr Babbercorn.

The vicar and the curate had an important meeting with the bishop that day, which they couldn't possibly miss. They weren't at all happy about sending the witches to London without them, but it couldn't be helped. Mendax and Alice were travelling with the witches, in a cat basket. Broomsticks would have attracted too much attention, so Mr Babbercorn had – reluctantly – decided they should go down on the train.

"Don't worry, Mr B.," said Skirty Marm cheerfully. They were all standing on the platform of the quiet country station, and Skirty Marm couldn't help looking forward to the adventure. "With any luck, you'll never see this snail again – because when we bring Alice back, she'll be a *person*."

"Do you remember all my instructions?" fussed Mr Snelling. "Is your money safe? And your packed lunch? Don't get the banknotes mixed up with the bat quiche – oh dear, why did that pesky bishop have to hold his meeting today?"

"No magic, unless it's to help Alice," Mr Babbercorn reminded them firmly. "No fighting, no jumping out of windows, no eating mice in public – are you *sure* you'll be all right?"

Old Noshie and Skirty Marm didn't reply. The London train was pulling into the station, and they had no eyes or ears for anything else. There are no railways on Witch Island, and the witches had never seen a train at close quarters. The size and speed of it amazed them. Once they were inside the train, the witches were deeply impressed by the bounciness of the seats.

Outside the window, the vicar and the curate carried on shouting advice, but the witches were too busy to listen. They were admiring their little table. Old Noshie immediately opened her packed lunch. Skirty Marm made her intellectual face, and opened a magazine called *Woman's Weekly*.

"I've written the vicarage phone number on top of Old Noshie's head!" shouted Mr Babbercorn. "If you get into trouble, just look under her wig!"

Slowly, the train began to move. The vicar and the curate waved until their arms ached. Mr Babbercorn stared after it until it was no more than a speck on the horizon.

"I *want* to trust them," he said gloomily, "but they've never been to a big city before, and you know how silly they can be."

"Mrs Miller did her best, but they still look absolutely bonkers, even in those clothes!" groaned Mr Snelling. "Oh, why have we let them do this?"

Mr Babbercorn sighed. "We must be bonkers ourselves, but what else can we do? We're counting on them to reverse that spell and bring Alice back!"

After they returned from the station, the vicar and the curate were too busy to be anxious. The bishop was coming for lunch, and the vicarage looked like the laboratory of a mad scientist. They had to work quickly to clear away all signs of spell-binding. Mr Snelling gathered up all the lost things that had arrived by mistake and took them into his study to sort through. Mr Babbercorn hid the witches' cauldron and wiped away the peculiar spillages.

He was sweeping a heap of dried spiders' legs into the dustpan when there was a loud knock on the back door. He opened it, and found himself staring up into the face of a gigantic woman.

She was nearly three metres tall, and nearly as wide. A shawl hid the lower half of her face, but the part you could see was incredibly ugly. She was holding a tray of red apples. Her mean little eyes glittered at Mr Babbercorn.

"Buy an apple, young reverend sir!" she wheedled. "Will you buy an apple to help a poor old woman?"

"I . . . I . . ." stammered Mr Babbercorn. Everything about this woman froze his blood. He knew why when her shawl fell down suddenly, revealing her mouth.

It was full of *metal teeth*!

"These are magical apples, young sir," cackled the old woman. "One bite and your dreams will come true!" The shawl fell further, revealing her chin.

It was covered with a *thick grey beard*!

At last, after all he'd heard about her, Mr Babbercorn was face to face with the wicked ex-queen of the Witches – Mrs Abercrombie

herself. His knees trembled and he felt the colour draining from his face, but he made his voice as strong as he could.

"Reverse that spell and give back my Alice, you inhuman FIEND!"

The change that came over Mrs Abercrombie's face when she realized she had been rumbled was very nasty. She stopped pretending. Her tray of apples vanished. And her smile turned into a hideous snarl.

"All right, so you're not as daft as Snow White, and you won't fall for the apple trick." She took a step nearer to the trembling curate. "You know what I want – and you'd better obey me if you want to see your Alice again. I've come for the Power Hat!"

"I . . . I haven't got it!" squeaked Mr Babbercorn. Which wasn't true – the Hat was in the spare bedroom upstairs, wrapped in an old sheet. He didn't dare think what would happen to his witches if the ex-queen got her hands on it.

"I know it's here," growled Mrs Abercrombie. "And I know your witch pals and that wretched cat-slave are away. You have no magic to protect you now!"

Mr Babbercorn did the only thing he could think of. With all the strength he could muster, he slammed the back door in Mrs Abercrombie's face.

"Locks and bolts cannot keep me out!" she thundered through the door. Her voice was deep and gravelly and seemed to shake the foundations of the house.

Mr Babbercorn hurtled upstairs to the spare bedroom and locked the door behind him.

"Good gracious!" he gasped. He rubbed his eyes to make sure he wasn't dreaming. Yesterday, the Power Hat had been covered with an old sheet. Today, it was covered with a cloth of gold, richly embroidered and studded with precious stones. The curate had never seen anything so beautiful – where had it come from? There was no time to wonder.

Downstairs, he heard a crash, followed by the voice of Mr Snelling.

"My good woman, what does this mean? How dare you smash down my back door? Leave my house this instant – OW! *Put me down*!"

Heavy footsteps came plodding up the stairs. Mrs Abercrombie was coming to claim her

Power Hat – and she would kill anything that stood in her way.

"Oh, crumbs – I know who you are now!" cried the voice of Mr Snelling, in sudden terror. "Cuthbert, don't let her in!"

This advice was pointless. Mrs Abercrombie bashed down the locked door as if it had been made of wet tissue paper. She was carrying the vicar over her shoulder.

"AT LAST! AT LAST!" she cried, with a great roar of triumph. "Months of work and all my fortune, but I've found my Hat! I am queen once more! Oh, come to me my proud beauty, and together we will reign in WICKEDNESS!"

She threw down the vicar (luckily, he landed on the spare bed) and tore aside the golden cloth that had recently been an old sheet. Her face lit up with horrible joy – and then an extraordinary thing happened.

Quick as lightning, the Power Hat leapt on to the head of Mr Babbercorn, burning a large hole in the ceiling. Mrs Abercrombie screamed and tried to snatch it back. But it wouldn't come off. She tugged, she pulled, she heaved. The Power Hat was stuck fast to the bewildered curate's head.

Mr Babbercorn now understood why Skirty Marm hadn't enjoyed wearing the Hat. It made his brain feel several sizes bigger, and so crammed with knowledge that it was about to burst. He shut his eyes and the strange letters appeared in the blackness inside his head.

Don't give me to that MONSTER! typed the Hat. *I don't want to be used for WICKED-NESS ever again. I have heard the playful sporting of the Brownies, and the wise counsel of the Old Folks' Club, and they have made me long to change! I have learnt how GOOD humans are, and I want to STAY!*

"Is that why all the strange things have been happening around you?" asked Mr Babbercorn. "The huge flowers, and our terrible choir singing like angels? Not to mention that old sheet turning to gold."

YES, typed the green letters. *These are the things I do now – I create sweetness and beauty. Think of all the beautiful things we could do together! Tell Mrs Abercrombie to GO AWAY. She has no power over you as long as I'm stuck to your head!*

Mr Babbercorn felt rather foolish, but did as he was told.

"The Hat says – well, I'm afraid it wants you to go away."

Mrs Abercrombie stamped her foot so hard that all the ornaments fell off the mantlepiece.

"I'LL BE BACK!" she screamed. "You've stolen my property! The Power Hat is rightfully MINE!"

And in a puff of black smoke that smelt of cabbage, she vanished.

Mr Snelling slowly got off the bed. He was shaking all over. "Bless my soul, that thing has discovered goodness! It wants to come and live in our village!"

Downstairs, the front doorbell rang.

"Oh dear," Mr Babbercorn said. "The bishop."

"You can't wear the Power Hat all through lunch with the bishop!" Mr Snelling was horrified. "He'll either think you've gone crazy, or he'll find out we're keeping witches on church property!"

"But I can't take it off!" protested Mr Babbercorn. He knew he couldn't possibly face his bishop in a two-metre-tall witch's hat with a candle at the tip.

He closed his eyes. "Hat – can you make

yourself look a little less strange?"

Certainly, typed the Hat. In half a second, it had changed itself into a small, woolly bobble hat. The hat was black, and the bobble was white.

"At least it's a *clergyman's* bobble hat," said Mr Snelling, relieved. "I'll tell him you've got a cold and you have to keep it on. But I wish I knew how the witches and Mendax and Alice were getting on in London!"

7

The Keepers of the Gate

"We're doing just *marvellously* so far," said Skirty Marm. "I can't think why the Vicar and Mr B. made all that fuss."

The witches were having the time of their lives. They had managed a thrilling journey on a train, an even more thrilling ride on the top of a red London bus, and now they were standing in front of the chocolate counter at Fortnum and Mason's.

It was five minutes before closing time, which was part of the plan. The famous shop was emptying, and the smart shop assistants were starting to close up their gleaming counters for the night. Some of them were looking curiously at the two peculiar old ladies with the cat basket, but they were far too polite to comment.

The voice of Mendax floated out of the basket, in a complaining mew. "We're supposed to be hiding – don't just stand there gawping!"

Mendax hadn't been having such a thrilling time. He'd been stuck in the cat basket with Alice all day, forbidden to speak in case a human heard him.

Old Noshie and Skirty Marm were still staring with open mouths at the magnificence around them. Skirty Marm took off her sunglasses to get a better view. It was an impressive sight, even for a human – great heaps of fruit, slabs of cheese, wonderful painted tins of biscuits and teas, and bottles of rare wine. It was nothing at all like the food hall at Maggot's, the only department store on Witch Island, where there was hardly anything for sale and you had to biff the assistants if you wanted to be served.

Mendax's voice reminded them they were here on a mission. Mr Snelling had drawn them a map of his favourite shop and suggested the basement as a good place to hide. Making sure nobody saw them, the witches scuttled down a grand staircase and found themselves in the hampers department, where big baskets of delicious food were sent out to customers. As the vicar had predicted, the biggest hamper was big enough to hide two witches and the cat basket. Its wicker sides creaked alarmingly as they climbed inside.

"It's a bit of a squeeze in here," complained Old Noshie.

"Serves you right," said Mendax. "Now you know what it's like to be shut in a basket."

"Let's not argue," peeped the tiny voice of Alice-the-Snail.

The others all remembered how terribly she wanted to stop being a snail, and how sad Mr Babbercorn would be if she stayed one. This made them very still and quiet, and Skirty Marm resisted the temptation to say something crushing to Mendax. Gradually, silence fell around them. The voices and footsteps seemed to go on for a very long time, but at last they were alone in the empty shop.

"Right," said Skirty Marm, clambering out of the hamper. "Let's get started." She put her sunglasses and her knitted hat into Mrs Miller's handbag. "Now, I'm going to try an aperture location spell to see if I can find the entrance that Professor Mouldypage talked about. We don't want to be stuck in here all night."

"I wouldn't mind," said Old Noshie, looking

hungrily at a pile of fruitcakes in tartan tins.

"You promised not to nick any food," Mendax reminded her smugly.

"We're not here to eat," Skirty Marm said impatiently. "The aperture location spell should lead us to the secret entrance to the Gardens Before Time, and then we can grab those berries Professor Mouldypage told us about."

Something had been worrying Old Noshie all day. Now that they were so close to the secret entrance, she couldn't help blurting it out. "Skirt – what did the Professor mean, when she said it might cost more than we were prepared to spend? I don't like the sound of that at all!"

"It probably means we have to pass some sort of test, or answer a tricky riddle," said Skirty Marm, who never liked to admit she didn't know something. "Don't worry – I'm brilliant at riddles."

"Supposing it's something dangerous?" quavered Old Noshie.

"Oh, it's bound to be dangerous," said Mendax. "I expect you'll have to walk through flames or over a bed of knives – or perhaps deal with a fierce dragon who might bite off your heads—"

"Shut up!" Skirty Marm stamped her foot. "It's too late to worry about the dangers now!"

She opened the cat basket. Mendax leapt out of it, with Alice-the-Snail clinging to the top of his head. Alice trembled as she watched Skirty Marm mumbling a long spell. Skirty snapped her fingers, and Alice gasped to see a round white light, about the size of a ping-pong ball, hovering in mid-air.

"It's searching," Old Noshie explained. "It's the aperture finder, and it will locate any magic within a radius of seven miles."

They all watched the white light anxiously. It moved slowly across the carpeted floor, over several glass cases and a large polished counter. Then, even more slowly, it came to a halt against a wall. It hung there for a moment, quivering like a dog sniffing, then dropped to the floor.

It stopped beside a metal grating in the wall and suddenly began to fizz like a firework, before disappearing in a shower of sparks.

"Hurrah!" yelled Skirty Marm, dancing a jig of excitement. "We've found it! That's the entrance!"

"But you'll never get inside that little hole!"

cried the tiny voice of Alice, in alarm. "You're miles too big!"

"My dear Alice," Mendax said, "you have a great deal to learn about magic. The witches will simply perform an elementary shrinking spell. I used it myself, to sneak out of the enemy camp at Fungus Gulch—"

"Shut up!" snapped Skirty Marm. She was trying to remember the shrinking spell, and secretly wishing she could look it up in her Red-Stocking Spellbook, which she'd had to leave behind on Witch Island.

Her first attempt shrunk everything except the witches' feet – Old Noshie let out a tremendous wail when she found her small body standing over a pair of feet as vast as a couple of tugboats.

Skirty Marm dealt Old Noshie a quick biff on the end of her huge shoe, which was the only part of her friend that she could reach. "Pull yourself together!" she ordered sternly.

Then Skirty Marm corrected her spell, and the witches' feet caught up with the rest of them. Their heads were now level with the worried snail clinging to Mendax's fur. The black cat himself looked the size of a carthorse beside them.

Together, they wrestled open the metal grating in the wall. Mendax slid his sleek cat's body through it. Alice clung on harder.

"I'm in a sort of pipe," Mendax said. His voice sounded strange and echoing. He sneezed. "Excuse me. It's rather dusty in here."

"Come on, Nosh." The shrunken Skirty Marm pushed Old Noshie through the grating, scrambled after her, and closed it behind them.

"It's awfully dark," squeaked Alice.

"You'd better light your finger, Skirt," said Old Noshie. "Whenever I try to do it, I end up setting fire to my wig."

Skirty Marm held out her finger, and a clear flame shot from the top of it. The dark pipe was flooded with light. The four of them stared at each other's frightened faces.

"What do we do next?" Alice-the-Snail asked fearfully.

"Walk on!" cried Skirty Marm. "Walk on, and the entrance will reveal itself!"

"You'd better climb on my back," said Mendax. "Please don't wriggle."

Skirty Marm vaulted easily up the cat's slippery black sides. Old Noshie was not such a good climber, and there was a delay while she was pulled up by her friend. It was extremely strange to be sitting on Mendax's smooth fur.

Very carefully, Mendax inched forward inside the metal pipe.

"Stop kicking!" he hissed crossly. "And there's no need to pull my fur out in handfuls!"

"I'm not!" protested Old Noshie. "How would you like it, if – OW!"

Without warning, the metal pipe seemed to melt from under Mendax's paws. The four of them were falling, falling, falling, into a pit of darkness. Old Noshie's borrowed wig flew off. Skirty Marm lost one of her human shoes. Still they went on falling, until they seemed to be plunging towards the very centre of the earth. It became very cold, then oddly warm.

At last, with a jolt that tumbled the witches off Mendax's back in a ragged heap, they landed on something hard.

They were in a dark underground cave, its walls and ceiling hidden by thick shadows. Something was gleaming at them, very brightly. When their eyes adjusted they saw a huge pair of golden gates, like spiders' webs, glistening in the flickering light of hundreds of candles.

Skirty Marm's eyes were round with awe. "The gates to the Gardens Before Time! No living witch has seen this incredible sight!"

A voice suddenly rang out, making the friends jump out of their skins. "Greetings, travellers!"

The voice was deep and rough, but strangely squeaky – and definitely not human.

"Welcome to the Chamber of the Order of the Good Rodents!"

Mendax turned white under his black fur. "Rodents? That means *rats*! They'll tear us to pieces!"

"Fear not, cat," said the voice. "You are safe with us."

Now they all saw that the darkness was studded with hundreds of pairs of beady eyes. They were surrounded by huge grey rats that were almost as large as Mendax. Alice screamed and shot back into her shell. Mendax cowered behind the two shrunken witches, who couldn't help looking nervous.

The largest of the rats stepped out into the candlelight. He wore a suit of rather rusty chain mail under a moth-eaten grey robe. His long tail was wrinkled and his whiskers were white with age, but his old voice was strong.

"We are the Order of the Good Rodents," he said. "Our Order was founded many thousands of years ago to guard this underground entrance to the Gardens Before Time. The Power Hat has prepared us for your coming."

"Power Hat?" muttered Skirty Marm, surprised. "Why on earth would it help us?"

"The Hat is not acting by itself," said the Chief Rat, in a deep and solemn squeak. "At the moment, it is stuck to the head of a very good young curate. He has ordered the Hat to help you. For this reason, we have waived the usual penalty."

"Eh?" gasped Old Noshie. There were too

many long words for her to understand.

The Chief Rat looked at her sternly, from beneath his bushy white eyebrows. "Know this, witch – usually, the berries from the Backwards tree are only given in exchange for a life. If you did not have such powerful friends, we would have been allowed TO EAT YOU."

Old Noshie's green face paled. "We taste horrible – don't we Skirt?" she said quickly.

"Now we know what the professor meant," said Skirty Marm, frowning. "Smelly old bag – she might have warned us properly!"

The Chief Rat turned his beady eyes towards her. "Would you have acted differently if you had known the true danger?"

"No!" Skirty Marm said bravely. "We'd do anything for Alice and Mr B. – we wouldn't even mind being eaten by rats!"

"Speak for yourself," muttered Mendax. "Personally, I'd have liked to be consulted first."

"You have our word," said the Chief Rat, "that you will not be eaten. This snail may enter the garden and remove two berries from the Backwards tree."

"Hooray!" cried Old Noshie. "Come on, Alice!"

The Chief Rat shook his grizzled old head. "The snail must enter on her own. Only she can be allowed to see the gardens – and live."

The witches and Mendax looked doubtfully at Alice, who seemed very small and delicate inside the circle of large grey rats. The little snail, however, came fully out of her shell and extended her horns. "Don't worry about me," she squeaked. "I'm not scared!"

"You love this curate," the Chief Rat said. His stern voice softened. "And your love will protect you as long as you remember to touch nothing else in the Gardens Before Time. Be warned, human female – if you even stop to rest on the way, you will stay in the gardens *forever*!"

"Oh, Alice, be careful!" wailed Old Noshie.

"I'm ready," said Alice bravely.

Alice found that she could move a lot faster than usual as she followed the Chief Rat towards the gleaming gates. He patted her shell once with his paw and unlocked the gates with a huge golden key. The witches and Mendax watched her sliding away alone into the shadows.

Skirty Marm nudged Old Noshie hard. "Stop crying!" she whispered, sounding cross because she was trying not to cry herself. Neither of them would ever forget the sight of tiny Alice, vanishing into the unknown.

"We will wait," said the Chief Rat. "Do sit down. And do have a biscuit – we get them from upstairs."

It was a long, long night. The witches and Mendax sat for uncountable hours, surrounded by silent staring rats. The biscuits were delicious, but even greedy Old Noshie was too anxious to enjoy them.

"Don't mind the others staring at you," said the Chief Rat. "They don't see many strangers."

"I'm not surprised!" snapped Mendax. "Word is bound to travel if you normally eat your guests!"

At last, the gate swung open. Old Noshie and Skirty Marm burst into cheers when the small snail emerged, carrying two purple berries in her horns. They rushed over to her.

"Are you all right?" cried Skirty Marm. "What happened?"

Alice-the-Snail's face was smiling in a dreamy dazed way.

"It was perfectly beautiful!" she sighed. "The

gardens are so sunny and quiet – I saw some angels having a picnic!"

"Yes, it's a popular spot," said the Chief Rat. "But I'd be grateful if you didn't tell anyone the details."

"I don't think I could if I tried," said Alice. "Thank you for being so kind to us."

For the first time, the Chief Rat smiled, his long sharp teeth gleaming in the darkness. "Don't mention it. Always a pleasure to oblige the Power Hat. And anyway, we've enjoyed it. You're the first visitors we've had in eight thousand years."

Alice said, "You must be awfully old!"

"As old as time, my dear," said the Chief Rat. "I watched time being wound up – and I'll stay here, guarding these gates, until it winds down."

Alice bowed her horns respectfully. "You've been very good. I'll never be mean about rats again!"

"Don't get carried away," said Mendax sourly. "Most of them are dreadfully common."

This seemed to amuse the old rat. "Cats and rats are not friends in the lands where time rules."

"The time!" cried Skirty Marm suddenly. "The vicar and Mr B. will be so worried! We've got to change Alice back!"

"We will escort you upstairs," said the Chief Rat. "Good luck – and if you want to send us a slice of your wedding cake, just drop it down any drain in Piccadilly."

8

Old Noshie's Dream Comes True

The journey back to the surface was so fast that it left them all breathless. They fell out of the grating in the hampers department in a heap, and Skirty Marm immediately changed herself and Old Noshie back to their proper sizes.

"Pity," remarked Mendax. "I liked you smaller."

"Now for the level six transforming spell," said Skirty Marm, ignoring him. She looked in Mrs Miller's handbag at the watch the vicar had lent her (Old Noshie hadn't been trusted with it because she couldn't tell the human time yet). "We'll have to be quick – there's only about an hour before the shop opens!"

Deciding this was an emergency, the witches borrowed a saucepan from the store's kitchen department and dashed around the shelves of the food hall snatching various ingredients.

"It's a good thing the professor said to leave out the warts," puffed Old Noshie, "because I don't think they have any!"

Skirty Marm had to concentrate very hard to perform the spell backwards, from end to beginning. The mixture in the saucepan looked disgusting – grey and curdled, with bits of squashed spider and grated geranium leaf floating on the scummy surface. Skirty lit all the fingers of her right hand and stuck them under the saucepan to bring it up to the boil. Mendax, Old Noshie and Alice watched, hardly daring to breathe, as she dropped in the two magic berries.

Above them, a door slammed.

"Someone's coming!" squealed Old Noshie. "Quick!"

As the mixture in the pan started to bubble there was a deafening crash, like a clap of thunder. It shook everything in the shop, and they felt the shudders deep in the earth beneath them. This was Mrs Abercrombie's locking charm unlocking. The blast sent the borrowed saucepan flying, and blew the friends off their feet.

While the witches were still coughing and

spluttering in the cloud of grey smoke, a woman's sweet voice cried, "Good gracious! I'm back!"

Mr Babbercorn and Mr Snelling hadn't slept a wink. They had sat up in the vicarage kitchen all night, drinking tea and trying to keep their spirits up. Both nearly jumped out of their skins when the phone rang.

"I knew it," groaned Mr Snelling. "It'll be PC Bloater – they've all been arrested! How are we going to explain this to the bishop?"

Mr Babbercorn answered the phone, and for the first time since Alice's transformation he laughed with joy.

"Alice!" he shouted.

Alice and her friends were at the station in Tranters End. Skirty Marm had made them all invisible to get them out of Fortnum and Mason's (and the man who opened the shop never could explain the huge explosion or the disgusting saucepan).

The vicar and the curate jumped into Mr Snelling's car and zoomed off to meet them. The other passengers on the small country station were amazed to see a young curate wearing pyjamas, a dog collar and a bobble hat dancing up and down the platform with two crazy old ladies, a cat and a woman in a blue dress.

With tears in her eyes, Alice hugged the witches and Mendax.

"How can we ever thank you all?" she cried. "Oh, Cuthbert – why on earth didn't you tell me about your magical friends straight away? They're WONDERFUL!"

Old Noshie and Skirty Marm were beaming. This was the proudest moment of their lives.

Mr Babbercorn gave them each a kiss. "It was stupid of me to hide you. I hope you'll forgive me."

The vicar sniffed and kissed Mendax – he loved the bossy little cat very dearly.

"Wait till you hear our adventures!" he said. "That blessed Power Hat wants to live in Cuthbert's underwear drawer! It wants to be good, and it will never give itself to Mrs Abercrombie again!"

"It seems to have taken rather a fancy to me," said Mr Babbercorn, smiling. "I've made it promise not to turn my vests into gold, like it did with the old sheet. Ordinary curates don't wear golden vests."

"Too itchy," put in Mr Snelling. "It says it'll prove its new goodness in quieter ways in future – and it's rebuilt my extension!"

Alice stroked Mendax and took the hands of the witches.

"Cuthbert," she said, "I'd like Mendax to sing a solo at our wedding. And I'd like these two lovely witches to be my bridesmaids!"

Old Noshie opened her mouth to say something – and not a sound came out. Her dream had come true.

Three weeks later, on a sunny summer afternoon, Mr Babbercorn and Alice were married. Mr Snelling took the service, with his round face wreathed in smiles. Every single person in Tranters End was crammed into the church.

"Don't they make a beautiful couple?" whispered Mrs Tucker.

Mrs Miller chuckled. "And don't those witches look a treat?"

Old Noshie and Skirty Marm walked behind the bride, holding up the train of her long white gown. Bridesmaids usually wear frilly dresses, but these hadn't been thought suitable for two rather wrinkled witches. Instead they had new

velvet dresses, with matching velvet-covered
pointed hats. Skirty Marm's were bright blue, to
set off her purple hair. Old Noshie was in
tasteful salmon-pink, to tone with her green
skin. They each carried a bouquet of thistles and
dandelions.

Mendax, who was very proud of his new
white collar, sang "O For the Wings of a Dove"
(licking his lips, because he was fond of a plump
dove).

"Skirt," said Old Noshie, "I'm the happiest witch in the world!"

"Me too," said Skirty Marm. "Pooh to Mrs Abercrombie – she can't touch the Power Hat now it wants to hide here. And she can't touch us, as long as it's here to protect us!"

Professor Mouldypage had sent a gleeful radio-message, telling them that the former queen had spent all her witch money on the locking charm and had now taken a job teaching at Yellow-Stocking School to make ends meet.

"So we'll all live happily ever after!" said Old Noshie.

When Mr and Mrs Babbercorn left for their honeymoon in Gusty Bay, Alice threw her bouquet of pink roses into the crowd – and Skirty Marm caught it.

Mr Snelling giggled. "That means you'll be the next bride!"

"Not likely," said Skirty Marm with a broad grin. "Being a bridesmaid's good enough for me." She bit the head off a rose. "DEE-LICIOUS!"

A selected list of titles available from Macmillan Children's Books

The prices shown below are correct at the time of going to press. However, Macmillan Publishers reserves the right to show new retail prices on covers which may differ from those previously advertised.

GWYNETH REES

Fairy Dust	0 330 41554 9	£4.99
Fairy Treasure	0 330 43730 5	£4.99
Fairy Dreams	0 330 43476 4	£4.99
Cosmo and the Magic Sneeze	1 405 05702 5	£9.99
Mermaid Magic	0 330 42632 X	£4.99

KATE SAUNDERS

Cat and the Stinkwater War	0 330 41576 X	£4.99

JEANNE WILLIS

Dumb Creatures	0 330 41804 1	£4.99
Rat Heaven	1 405 02068 7	£9.99

All Pan Macmillan titles can be ordered from our website, www.panmacmillan.com, or from your local bookshop and are also available by post from:

Bookpost
PO Box 29, Douglas, Isle of Man IM99 1BQ

Credit cards accepted. For details:
Telephone: +44(0)1624 677237
Fax: +44(0)1624 670923
Email: bookshop@enterprise.net
www.bookpost.co.uk

Free postage and packing in the UK.